# The Solar Eclipse
**A James Anderson Mystery**

# The Solar Eclipse

## A James Anderson Mystery

Samantha Sudol

All rights reserved. Published in the United States by Elnath Publishing, New Jersey.

First edition June 2023
Front cover image by Sabrina Sudol

Library of Congress Control Number: 2023903779

Hardcover ISBN: 979-8-9862944-0-7
Paperback ISBN: 979-8-9862944-1-4
Ebook ISBN: 979-8-9862944-2-1

*For my family and friends*

# Contents

# Chapter One

It was early in the morning when men dressed in bowler hats and thick scarves turned the streetlights on again. James Anderson was sitting on a park bench next to his viridian Alcyon Windsor bicycle when he noticed the men lighting the bulbs, preparing for the celestial oddity. He looked at the newsboy across the street holding folded copies of the *New York Times*. The headline crunched under his arm in large bold letters:

*FIRST TOTAL SOLAR ECLIPSE IN NEARLY 450 YEARS.*

The eclipse was due to take place around nine that morning. James checked his watch—quarter past seven. It would only be a little while longer until the city would be consumed in the darkness that came from the moon blotting out the sun. Astronomers thought the path of totality for this 1925 eclipse would begin at the northern edge of Manhattan. The path would run through the city in a way that would allow observers from 96th Street and above to see the totality, while those underneath the direct path would only see the eclipse partially.

People littered the streets, their usual weekday routine abandoned. Vendors in knitted shawls with cigarette-stained teeth held shards of smoked glass in their calloused hands, trying to sell to the people who walked by. James got off the bench and pulled his navy blue jacket closer around him, hurrying as one of the vendors with greasy black hair bumbled over to him.

"Save your eyes for twenty cents!" the man yelled over the relentless wind that raked through his hair.

James hiked one leg over his bike to sit on the molded leather seat. "I'm all set," he called out, seeing the gears in the vendor's mind spin.

The man's calculating smile resembled a checkerboard, as a few teeth were missing. "How about ten cents, just for you. You can't be missing this."

James smiled and refused again, pushing one foot against the raised pedal and using the other to kick off the pavement. He didn't mind cycling to work in the morning, the station wasn't too far. Besides, today he enjoyed seeing the crowd prematurely looking through their opera glasses and eyepieces as they made their way uptown. Other onlookers hailed taxis from the curb or rode in horse-drawn carriages to find the perfect vantage point for the eclipse.

As he rode down the sidewalk, he weaved through the mob, the yellow rims of his wheels standing out against their mundane coats as he went by. Once he reached 135th Street in Harlem, he turned left and crossed the road, gliding down the street to the 32nd Precinct of the New York Police Department. He got off his bike once his speed lessened, looking up at the magnificent four-story building.

Twin lanterns shined a pale light against the large wooden door.

James walked down the side of the building to lock up his bicycle, noting the bare limbs of the trees behind the station. After completing his task, he walked into headquarters. He nodded in acknowledgement to his colleagues, clad in their long-sleeved felt jackets, as he walked through the hall. Each uniform had ten silver buttons and a thick collar, with badges neatly pinned over the left breast with their force identification number. A hand slapped James on the back.

"Nice one, James. Finally got some bracelets on that bearcat. Took you long enough." Detective Tony Fiore elbowed James in the ribs, his stocky frame causing more damage than intended.

James grimaced. "Figured it was about time. Have I missed her mugging?"

"Only just. Armande put up a fight in the gymnasium. Michaels and I had to drag her across the stage to get her into the studio for the picture."

James thought about the studio, which illuminated those arrested and created a hard, dead-white glare that almost made the skin look swollen and ragged, adding an unnecessary purple hue that made the person look more like a corpse in their photo. "Was she fingerprinted too?"

"Yes, sir," Tony said, pride highlighting his round face. "And we seized her gang's weapons when we picked them up this morning. Those are at the bottom of the sea now, dumped into the Narrows between Brooklyn and Staten Island.

"Good. Is there anything left to do on the Spades case?" James asked.

"I reckon that's all. Michaels wants to see you though."

Tony paused for a moment. "Hey, where were you anyway? This being your big moment and all."

James wrung out his wrists. "I had other duties to attend to. Besides, I'd rather not be behind the eight ball, if you know what I mean. I don't want any more trouble with that group."

Tony snorted. "Why that's baloney. She won't be out of the big house for a long while. You just didn't want to get a pretty girl in trouble, you softie."

James looked away. "Where is Michaels? I shouldn't keep him waiting."

"He's in his office." Tony relaxed his shoulders and checked his watch. "I better get going myself. Seems to be a problem down by Riverbank State Park."

James checked his watch and saw it was a few minutes past eight. "You're just trying to get a good spot for the eclipse," he teased.

Tony put his hands up. "You got me. Don't be jealous I thought of an excuse to get out of here for a while before you did."

James shook his head and turned to walk down the hall to Michaels's office. He rapped his knuckles against the wooden door that had CHIEF OF POLICE painted on the fogged glass.

"Come in," a voice croaked.

James pushed open the door and found the chief at his desk. Chief Michaels was a small man, in his sixties, with a wistful mouth and a patch of silver hair on his head. The room wasn't expansive, with only a single window, desk, and a few filing cabinets. Papers were splayed across the desktop, with a collection of black pens neatly stashed in a mason jar.

"You asked to see me, sir?" James said, wiping his palms against his pants.

"I did." Michaels stood, leaning his thin frame across the desk. "Inspector Harlan spoke highly of you in the Spades case." He fingered through the edges of the papers before him.

"That's very generous, sir. I was just following orders."

"Just the same. It was a job well done." Michaels lifted a piece of paper from the pile. "Here we are. I received a letter this morning from an Inspector Evans."

James pinched his lips together, his face paling.

Michaels's birdlike eyes traced the expression on James's face. "Curious, very curious. What does this inspector hold over you?"

"Nothing, sir."

Michaels remained still a moment before nodding. "Good." He flipped the letter over in his scarred hands. "I'm afraid to say that despite my best effort of keeping you here, it has been decided you will be transferring back to the Conway division in New Hampshire. Evans believes you have some work that needs to be done up there."

Michaels squinted at James, waiting for him to say anything, but James stood dumbfounded.

The chief let out a sigh. "Can't say that I blame Evans. You have been an invaluable asset on our team this year." Michaels folded the letter in his hands before sitting back onto his chair, stroking the paper in thought. "Why would Evans request you back so urgently?"

James shrugged. "Don't I have a say in any of this? Going back, I mean."

"Duty calls, Anderson. You'll be leaving tonight for North Conway. That is final."

James raised his brow. "Tonight? I haven't made any arrangements. And there aren't any trains going directly to North Conway."

Michaels raised a hand. "Calm down. I pulled some

strings and spoke to a buddy of mine. Fortunately, he's willing to add you and O'Reilly aboard his train."

"O'Reilly?" James asked.

"O'Reilly from the newspaper. He wants to write a story on Elizabeth Kingston, who will also be boarding with you."

"What kind of train is taking celebrities directly to North Conway?"

"A private one. Alexander Cross owns *The Blue Star*."

"What's the catch? What position are you in to ask him this kind of favor?"

"Never you mind. I'll have O'Reilly pick you up at seven in front of Girard's. Don't be late. Until then, you are dismissed." Michaels gestured for James to leave the room as he refocused his attention to the other documents on his desk.

It only took James a few minutes to race back to Graham Court, an apartment building between 116th and 117th Street he'd called home for the past year. At eight-stories tall, the building was designed with an Italian palazzo in mind. This cube-like structure had its bottom two floors made from rusticated limestone, tan brick above that, with a crowning story of foliate terra-cotta and a cornice of copper. After locking his bike by the entrance of the building, James walked under the entryway arch, the name Graham Court engraved into the stone. James was only living here briefly, having been tasked with figuring out how to halt the activities of the nefarious jewel thief Juliette Armande and her club, The Silver Spades, who lived there.

James entered the grand lobby and entered the elevator

to the left. He looked at the new manual elevator controls and pushed the knob for the fourth floor. Due to the elevator operators strike in 1920, self-service elevators had been installed in the building. He looked into the corner, where the old operator's handle stood, having been mounted upright on the elevator wall. Once the elevator reached his floor, he stepped out and turned left down the hall. At room 425, he took out the key from his pocket and shoved it into the lock until it clicked, the door moaning as it opened into the mosaic-floored foyer.

James dropped his key into a woven basket on the entryway table and picked up the smoked glass he'd bought a week prior. He went further into the large apartment, the floor turning into a rich mahogany wood. An open window from the parlor pulled in a stream of cold air, and as he moved toward it, he checked his watch. With only a couple of minutes until the totality, he put the glass up to his eyes, looking skyward as the moon fronted the sun and a shadow fell over New York.

# Chapter Two

J ames was washing up after his early dinner when he heard the phone ring. He slid the checkered dish towel through the silver loop that held it and moved toward the whirring sound, the floorboards creaking under his body weight. He gripped the candlestick base to position the mouthpiece before taking the receiver to his ear.

"Is this James Anderson? It's Inspector Evans from the Conway Police."

He didn't speak, letting the wind that shook the building answer for him.

"Is this or is this not James Anderson? I haven't got all day."

James cursed under his breath. "What do you want?"

"Where the Hell have you been? We were all worried sick when you just—"

"If you were calling out of concern, you would have found me months ago. So why now? What could you possibly want from me." His voice was steady, numb.

The inspector let out a grunt. "We got a letter down

here at the station for you. It's urgent and I need you up here immediately. I'll meet you at the train station when you arrive."

"You can't order me around anymore. I told you when I left that I was not coming back. I had to leave; you should understand that better than anyone." James ripped the receiver from his ear and threw it against the bookcase. The wire attaching the receiver to the mouthpiece pulled it from his hand, following in a volley. Upon impact, books tumbled from their carefully chosen spots, landing in a heap on the floor. He tried to close his eyes and breathe in deeply but failed to stop the twitching that took over his hands, like ants running up and down his nerves.

A couple of raindrops from a leak in the ceiling fell on his shoulder as he hesitantly picked up the receiver and mouthpiece.

"Who is it from, the letter?"

"That's what I'm trying to tell you. It's from your father. From Caiden."

"I know you better than that. You wouldn't call after all this time for a lousy letter."

"I can't talk about it on the phone. You are the closest link we have to finding out what happened to—"

"Don't say her name." James's emerald green eyes darted toward the window. Concentrating on a raindrop falling from the top of the frame, he watched it roll down the misty glass. Through the rain, the evening lights flickered in the street below, while businessmen in their long black coats and hats tried desperately to keep their umbrellas from swaying back and forth in the merciless wind.

"Listen." The inspector's voice softened. "After you left, I asked Caiden to do some digging. He said he might be able to help us find out what happened to her, but he has to speak with you first. I've never asked anything of you, but for God's sake, get on that train."

James closed his eyes, allowing the silence to absorb him.

"Come home," the inspector repeated.

James heard the phone call end and placed the receiver on the hilt that connected it to the mouthpiece. He crouched to pick up the books that had fallen. Reaching first for the heavily worn spine of *Alice's Adventures in Wonderland*, the novel opened to a dog-eared page as he pulled the book in front of him. Within the text was a thick underline in black ink.

> *When the day becomes the night and the sky becomes the sea,*
> *when the clock strikes heavy and there's no time for tea;*
> *and in our darkest hour, before my final rhyme, she will*
> *come back home to Wonderland and turn back the hands*
> *of time.*

He closed the book delicately, then tucked it under his arm and walked into his bedroom.

Taking an old leather suitcase from his closet, he tossed it onto the rickety bed. The bedsprings played a flat melody against the chorus of rain that landed heavy blows against the side of his apartment. Without giving it much thought, he tossed an assortment of clothing into the case, then retrieved his Dopp kit from the bathroom. He wrapped his calloused fingers around the suitcase handle, then pulled his worn coat tighter around him before walking out the front door.

Reaching the street, the dark gray sky hung low as it wept, turning James's copper-colored hair into a shaggy, dirty blond. Heavy raindrops shot into James's coat like liquid bullets. He kept his chin tucked against the collar of his shirt to find some warmth, his downturned eyes watching the rainwater rush from the sidewalk and pour into the sewers. The sounds of car horns and street traffic filled the air. He looked up to the street signs briefly before continuing to 115th Street, where he was told O'Reilly would be picking him up for the twenty-minute car ride to the station.

Reaching the corner faster than he had intended, James slowed his pace and noticed the pungent smell of sharp cheddar cheese and pumpernickel bread that wafted its way from the kitchens of the nearby restaurants on the street. He felt a knot form in his stomach and focused instead on staying dry as he waited under a golden awning with large crimson letters: Girard's. He let his back fall against the brick wall and felt his eyelids begin to droop.

He was snapped awake by a blaring horn.

"Hey you! Anderson," a voice called from the street.

James scanned the rush of traffic as he turned toward the direction of the voice. A large man with hair stiffer than a hair pin was waving him over. James hurried to the car and pulled the door open.

"Are you Mr. O'Reilly, from the paper?"

The man beamed. "One and the same. You can call me Martin." Martin lit a cigarette. "Well come on, get in. Seems like I'm playing chauffeur today."

James climbed into the car and threw his suitcase onto the back seat.

Martin took a puff of his cigarette while steering the car back into the street. "Ever drive one of these things? I just picked up this Tin Lizzie from Hamilton Heights."

"I haven't," James huffed, returning his gaze to the congested road.

Martin turned to analyze James's reaction, then pushed his cigarette to the other side of his mouth. "Not much of a talker, are ya. How long have you been here? In New York, I mean."

"About a year." James replied, pushing his hair back into place from where the rain had slicked it down.

"I figured you were pretty new around these parts if you haven't had the chance to drive one of these. Or perhaps Michaels just doesn't like you." Martin snickered.

James looked away, catching his reflection in the car mirror.

"I've lived here my whole life. You hate it, you love it. I go back and forth," Martin continued nonchalantly. "I'm going to park this beaut' in the Acton lot. I'll have someone pick her up in the morning and drive her back to the station." Martin moved his cigarette to his left hand and drove the car with his elbow as he used his other hand to pull two crumpled train tickets out of his pocket. "You can hold on to the tickets if you want."

James took the tickets and flattened them against his wrinkly pants. He scanned the small pieces of paper. Across the top of the tickets, in a mesmerizing golden script, read *The Blue Star*.

"We're lucky Michaels was able to get us on board." James said.

Martin snorted. "Is that what he told ya? Ha! I was the one who got us the tickets." He let out a puff of smoke through his knobby teeth. "I need to meet with a client to get the scoop on her newest record. It just so happens she will be boarding *The Blue Star* with her manager. It's his personal train, these tickets are only for show. You're a lucky bastard to even get a chance to take this ride, but I was owed the favor." Martin winked, waiting for any indication of gratitude.

Met with silence, he continued. "This isn't just any trip,

you know. The family who owns the train prides themselves on their exceptional food and atmosphere."

"Where did you hear that?" James asked. Suddenly his body slammed forward, and he put his hands out in front of him to brace against the dash as Martin slammed on the brakes.

"What the Hell?" Martin bellowed, his knuckles turning a chalk white as he gripped the steering wheel.

James bit his cheek as he watched the tail end of the car that had cut them off disappear down the road. "The parking garage is just off of 45th if you take this right here." He motioned with his hand to the right.

"I know where I'm going," Martin growled, turning the car to the right. Constructed in the famous French beaux-arts style, the Acton Garage stood three stories high and was made entirely from light brown bricks. The second and third floors had six windows each, aligned horizontally in pairs of two. The pitch-black paint of the garage doors contrasted starkly against the light exterior of the building.

Martin rolled down the window and threw his cigarette into the road before continuing to the entrance. The attendant, whose clothes began to stick to his thin torso like paper as he stepped out into the rain, tilted his badge in their direction as he made his way over to speak to Martin.

"How long are the two of you going to be gone?"

"I'm going to send someone to come pick her up tonight; the kid's name is Billy Whitman."

Martin and James watched as the man walked back inside to write down the details before returning a moment later.

"Alright, sir. Please sign this and everything else will be taken care of."

Martin reached for the paper and pen and signed his name quickly in black ink, leaving the paper on the seat as he exited the automobile. James followed suit and walked to the back of the car for Martin to collect his luggage from the back seat.

"Grab hold of those," Martin demanded, gesturing toward his luggage.

James rolled his eyes as he reached to take hold of the black leather bags, combining them with his old beat-up case. He grunted after feeling the weight. "Jesus, what do you have in here?"

"That isn't any of your business, Anderson," Martin snapped. "Let's get going. We can't afford to be late."

Once the key had been handed over, they walked briskly toward Grand Central Station, located a few streets south on 42nd. As they got closer, the limestone and granite of the station reflected the streetlights down Park Avenue. White columns adorned the exterior in pairs on either side of the towering windows. The windows themselves were framed in dramatic archways, like those of a palace. The top of Grand Central was adorned by the Roman Gods Mercury and Hercules, and Goddess Minerva. It would have appeared that time stood still were it not for the clock that restlessly kept marching onward through the minutes and hours. Underneath the clock, the name Grand Central was carved into the thick stone.

James and Martin walked underneath the statue of Cornelius Vanderbilt.

"It's almost unsettling to think I won't be back for a while," James mumbled.

"The City Beautiful movement worked overtime to make sure this wouldn't fall into disrepair. I'm sure you will be back before it does." Martin patted the stone with his free hand before turning to make sure James was keeping pace.

As they walked through the station and approached the

boarding area, Martin held on to the handrail to descend to the platform. Placing their suitcases on the jagged concrete, James looked around for other passengers to come down the steps for the 8:00 p.m. train on the adjacent track, but they were alone. His ears perked up upon hearing the shrill of a train whistle, and James walked toward the track expectantly. Soon enough, a silver train rushed past them into the station, the deep blue compartments flying by so that it was impossible to make out the gold lettering underneath the windows. James pushed his hand into his pocket to feel the crisp, smooth edge of the ticket, raising his other hand to shield his eyes from the fumes.

When the train came to a halt, James saw the golden streaks transformed into letters: The Blue Star. When the train had slowed and halted, two men dressed in pale blue uniforms with silver buttons pulled open the thin door. The porter jumped off the train in one swift movement and made his way toward them, while the conductor, a stout man with a receding hairline and thick eyebrows, adjusted his hat as he waited in the entryway of the door.

"Are you the two boarding?" the porter asked, looking to either side of Martin.

"Sorry to disappoint you, but yes, it will just be us." Martin handed the porter one of his suitcases. "Handle these with the utmost care, not that I think it would be an issue or anything." Martin winked as he passed James and went into the train. The conductor moved to the side to let him pass, then followed him aboard to take him to his compartment.

"I'm sorry about him," James said to the porter. "He has a lot on his mind. I can help you with his bags, all I've got is this one right here." He brought his suitcase closer to his chest.

"That won't be necessary, sir," the young porter responded while he straightened his gloves and lifted Martin's bags.

"Call me James, please." He picked up the bags that were left and carried them into the train. After dropping off the rest of Martin's things, James looked into the grandeur of the dining coach next to Martin's room.

In the hallway, the conductor scratched his chin thoughtfully before reaching into his pocket and handing the porter a key. "Put Mr. Anderson in room 5B, Dean," he said. "I already put Mr. O'Reilly here in 6A."

Dean nodded, then led the way down the hall to the next car, stopping in front of a door marked 5B. He pulled a small brass key from the breast pocket of his waistcoat and handed it to James. "We only have one guest key for each room, so don't lose it," the young man informed James, then headed toward the front of the train.

Twirling the fine swirled brass key between his fingers, James placed it in the keyhole, then swung open the door. He was taken aback by his compartment—ruby carpeted floor and dark wooden walls adorned with two silver luggage racks. He placed his suitcase on one rack and looked out the window as the train left the station. James took off his coat and unlatched his suitcase to pull out a book, leaving the rest of his luggage disarrayed, and settled in to read. The weight of the book, the well-read copy of *Alice's Adventures in Wonderland*, felt comforting in his hands as he picked through the pages. Artistic handwriting filled the margins—lost thoughts immortalized in pen.

Finding the silence unsettling after a time, he closed the book and went to look around. While he was walking the train, they reached Long Island, New York, a stop the train was only making to collect the celebrity Elizabeth Kingston. From the paper, James knew her as a rising singer and fashion icon who was in her early twenties. And while her name was only beginning to be studded in lights, she was set to begin a tour around New England using this glamorous private train. The notoriety was good business, or so it was perceived.

James walked past Martin, who stood in the doorway of his compartment, a small black Vest Pocket Autographic Kodak camera in his hands as he aimed to catch a picture of Miss Kingston.

"Get ready for this headline. I hope it will make the front page," Martin said with confidence.

James shrugged. "There are a lot more interesting topics."

"Don't be such a spoilsport." Martin gripped the doorframe as the train slowed upon approaching the platform.

It was impossible to miss the entourage and flashing lights that had followed Elizabeth onto the platform. Flaunting a white fur coat and shimmering golden heels, she was like a lighthouse to those lost in a dark, stormy sea. Once the train came to a complete halt, the conductor opened the door. Dean hopped out to help with her candy pink bags, which looked surprisingly heavy as he carried them onto the train and into her compartment across from the master suite of 1A. James could hear dozens of cameras clicking away as the photographers shouted at her.

"Look here! The camera can't get enough of ya," said one man in a brown trench coat, his pipe slanted across his lips.

"Why don't you give us a kiss?" another man said.

"Come now," Elizabeth said as she brought her purse closer to her chest. She winked, then grabbed the rail of the luxury car and pulled herself up the stairs, her long white coat dancing in the wind. Martin closed the door behind her after she passed.

"Why thank you, darling." Elizabeth flashed a crescent smile as she opened her compartment door and entered.

Once the train began to move again, Martin grasped James's shoulder. "I'm going to need you to pull your weight."

"I don't think I need to be doing anything for you." James said.

"It's about Miss Kingston. I need you to help me get close to her."

James gave him a blank look.

"Oh, come on, haven't you read the news? Elizabeth might be changing managers, which is a huge controversy."

James ran a hand through his hair. "I don't have time for these unnecessary dramatics."

"Hey, I make money off of unnecessary dramatics."

"Then you'll know how to get what you want," James said, a smile dangling from his lips.

Martin winked. "You have no idea."

At the sound of footsteps, the men turned to see a petite woman who couldn't have been older than twenty, her dark hair neatly pinned in a bun.

"What is it?" Martin asked, crossing his arms.

"Dinner is ready," she quickly replied, tucking her thin hands into her apron.

James nodded and watched as she scurried off to the next compartment.

"So, you know your way around North Conway?" Martin asked.

"More than I'd care to admit. I used to live there with my father." James furrowed his brow, lost in thought.

"Well, there is nothing I like more than a good homecoming. I'm sure your folks will be glad to see you."

James grimaced. "Come on, we shouldn't keep our host waiting."

Upon entering the dining coach, James stopped for a moment to let Dean walk past, a silver platter of colored drinks in his hand. Martin abandoned James to follow the alluring Elizabeth. She had changed into a short, silver dress with a shallow scoop neckline and a cutout in the middle the shape of a teardrop. The dress was sleeveless except for the two-inch-wide straps that held it in place. Golden threaded spirals decorated the garment, as well as small crystals that caught the light. The bottom of the dress shredded into silver and gold fringe that went down to her knees. The loose threads followed her graceful movements as she walked to turn on the radio. With a flick of her painted finger, light jazz music filled the air.

"Drink, sir?" asked Dean, a kaleidoscope of liquor swirling on his platter.

James shook his head. "No, thanks."

Dean made a slight bow before walking toward the other passengers, his eyes fixed on James as he walked away.

Looking around the compartment, James was surprised to see just a handful of passengers scattered around the room. He walked over to the bar, where Martin was already on his second drink. Elizabeth approached James and touched his shoulder.

"You must be Mr. Anderson. Martin was just telling us about you." She kissed his cheek lightly before taking a drink off a nearby tray and handing it to him.

James smiled and took it politely, watching Martin turn back to face the bar.

James's attention stayed with Elizabeth as she received

a man on her right, and he watched her blue eyes spark with familiarity. The tall man had a smooth jawline paired with a rounded chin. He had a widow's peak, and his neatly trimmed auburn hair framed brooding chestnut eyes. Clad in a double-breasted gray suit with pinstripes, his dark red tie made him stand out amongst the men. He made his way next to Elizabeth and placed a hand on her forearm, revealing a golden laurel art deco style wedding band on his left ring finger.

Elizabeth placed a hand on top of his, then turned back to James. "It is my pleasure to introduce Mr. Alexander Cross."

Alexander extended his hand to James, who shook it.

"And you are?" Alexander asked.

"James Anderson."

"Nice to meet you, James. I hope you enjoy your time on board."

"Thank you. Your Pullman compartments are exquisite," James said, motioning to the dark oak carvings on the wall next to him.

"At last, someone else gets to appreciate the fine work put into this contraption. My father originally bought it, so it has been in the family for some time. Fiona insisted we add on the bells and whistles, and with my brother being a train enthusiast, I encouraged it. Now with the present circumstances, I don't know how much longer it will be before we sell it."

"Present circumstances?"

"Oh, you wouldn't understand."

James shrugged. "Try me."

Alexander shook his head and conceded. "Well, let's just say when Chief Michaels called and paid for us to host Martin and yourself, we were delighted. The extra press doesn't hurt either. Besides, Roger and I have business in

Conway." Alexander grinned. "At any rate, I must speak to the others."

Alexander and Elizabeth left to make their way around to greet the other guests. James placed his glass on a nearby tray, took a seat at the bar next to Martin, and ordered a highball.

Martin sneered. "I didn't take you as a man who would order such a drink."

James was about to reply when he caught a man staring at him from across the bar. He had angular features, a piercing jawline, and a blunt, square chin. He also had the same chestnut eyes as Alexander, but his hair was jet-black and coated in grease.

Martin shoved James's shoulder lightly to break the spell. "That's Roger Cross, Alexander's younger brother."

James's eyes widened with disbelief. "You've got to be joking. They're like night and day."

"Don't discredit him. Alexander may be more likable, but Roger isn't trying to sell you an image. What is far more interesting is that catfight." Martin nodded his head in the direction of two women, their voices steadily rising. He chugged his drink before walking over to the two.

James followed.

The louder of the two was a small woman with dark brown hair and hazel eyes. While she was the shortest of everyone in the room, there was a fire about her that told James she wouldn't back down from any argument without a fight.

"James, I would like you to meet Mrs. O'Donnell," said Martin.

She was wearing a sheath-like shimmering green dress that traced her figure. The bottom was lined with white fur. She held her head high with authority. "There is no need to be so formal, Martin," She turned to look up at James.

"It's nice to meet you. Please call me Clara." She smiled at James, then looked back at her debate partner.

Unlike Clara, this woman was tall and willowy, with long wavy blonde hair that fell like a waterfall over her dark blue evening dress. The dress had mesh long sleeves with a golden hand-stitched design that matched the design at the base of the dress, which draped down to her ankles. James followed her gaze as she watched Alexander leave the compartment with his hand around Elizabeth's waist. She then turned her sapphire eyes to James.

"Fiona Cross. Pleased to make your acquaintance."

Martin looked amongst the party. "If you wouldn't mind, Clara, might I have a word?"

Clara's cheeks flushed a soft pink. "Of course, Martin."

James watched Martin and Clara leave, then escorted Fiona to a small oak table in the corner of the compartment.

"I spoke to Alexander earlier. He said you had business up North?" James asked, trying to strike up a conversation.

Fiona smiled faintly. "We are going to my mother-in-law's estate in New Hampshire."

"Do you visit her often?"

"Yes, although Alexander has been pretty busy with his work of late."

"What does he do?"

"He's a talent agent. He met Miss Kingston two years ago. Some would say he is married to his work."

"How long have you been married?"

"Oh, many years now. They all bleed together. Are you married?"

James folded his hands on the table. "It's complicated."

"There is no rush. Marriage isn't always what it's made out to be." She put her hand on top of his. "Trust me on that."

# Chapter Three

As the night wound down, James wished his companions well before retiring to his compartment. Pulling out the key from his pocket, he opened the door to find that while he was away Dean had reconfigured the room. The red booth next to the train window he had sat in earlier while reading had been transformed into a bed for the night. James changed into more casual attire before sitting on the bed. Using the heat of his hand, he defrosted a part of the window to look up at the stars. Straining his eyes, he could vaguely distinguish the constellation of Capricorn. James picked up his pocket watch from the side table to check the time; it was 1:00 a.m. He carefully placed the watch back on the table before lying down. Besides the sound of the train wheels violently turning beneath him, the train was quiet.

James started to close his eyes but changed his mind. Falling asleep would only make it easier for him to visualize her. The way her long locks were matted in blood streaming from the side of her head. Or how her clothes stuck to her body after being recovered from the lake. The thin smile she wore as the light faded from her glassy eyes, exhaling her last breath.

Looking into the dark hallway as he thought, he saw Martin running past, the glass walleye lens of his flashlight illuminating the hall. James, happy with any distraction, unlocked his door and poked his head into the hallway.

"Is everything alright?" he called after Martin.

Martin turned around, beaming his flashlight at James. "Great, I found you. Come with me."

James squinted from the light, trying to navigate his way to putting on his coat and shoes. He walked hesitantly into the hall, his eyes readjusting as Martin moved down the cold, dark passage. James picked up the pace to stay within arm's length.

"What is going on?" he asked, hoping Martin would have more to say.

Martin stopped abruptly in front of an open door, causing James to nearly crash into him. He turned to James, his wild eyes darting between James and both ends of the hallway, then put his forefinger over his lips. He shifted his weight and tightened his grip around the flashlight. A sharp creak from the floorboards shattered the silence, causing James's body to pulse with adrenaline. Martin flicked the light switch on, eerily loud in the space.

James squinted as he entered. As soon as he stepped onto the beige carpeting, the dense smell of iron flooded his nose. The turquoise walls, ornamented with pictures and paintings each more glamorous than the next, were streaked with blood. A priceless vanity dressed the opposing wall, ornate wood carvings of cupid and cherubs surrounding the mirror. The gems and jewelry that used to be protected inside were scattered around the legs of the furniture like ornaments off a fallen Christmas tree. The centerpiece of the room, a wooden desk made of stained oak, was devoid of its stature, its grandeur marred by the dripping blood that buried itself into the carpet. Martin pulled out his camera, his flash lighting up the room to immortalize the gruesome scene.

James felt his throat tightening. He clenched his fists, closed his eyes, and leaned against the compartment wall. He felt the melody of the train wheels harshly purring on the track. Martin continued to disrupt the song through bursts of flash, surrounding the room in sheets of white.

Regaining his composure, James pushed past Martin and knelt next to the lifeless woman on the floor, her bright blonde hair framed crimson in a crown of blood. Fiona's blue eyes were open, frozen in fear as she realized this was the last moment of her life. James used the back of his hand to delicately close her eyelids. As James stood up, he noticed how her blue dress was turning a dark violet. He knelt again and tried to examine her body, hoping to figure out how many times she'd been stabbed. Martin remained quiet as James uncovered the marks that painted her torso a dark red, black, and blue. It didn't require a detective to know this was a crime of passion.

"James, you might want to look at that." Martin pointed at Fiona's arm.

James looked at the peculiar mark across the back of her bicep. His eyes widened. Despite years in the police force, he'd never seen anything like it. These weren't just a series of cuts, rather, they were numbers carved into her skin. James asked to borrow a notebook and pen from Martin and quickly wrote down the numbers that were becoming illegible, swallowed by her blood—71200.

James cleared his throat before he spoke. "We need to get help."

"We could ask the conductor to stop in Hartford, then

I can mail them to my editor for the story. He will develop them faster." Martin played with the lens on his camera.

"We need to stop as soon as we can; if Hartford is closest, then so be it." James paused, scrutinizing the man. "You know you can't publish these until the case is solved. If we send them to an editor, they won't escape the morning news."

"We need to get this story out there. Maybe someone will know something."

"Out there? We're on a moving train. No. Everyone we need right now is here. This must stay internal."

Martin retreated to the corner of the room, his nostrils flaring. "I need this story. It's my job to report what I see and hear. I have the right as an American—"

"Have a heart." James crossed his arms, slowly examining the bloody room. "I can't stop you from publishing, but wouldn't you rather wait until we know who did it? No one wants to read a mystery without a proper ending." James bent over to pick at the silver and gold jewelry on the floor, gathering them in his hands before pouring them onto the vanity.

Martin rested his chin on his chubby fingers. "Fine. I'll hold off until it's solved then. But I swear, if someone else publishes first, it'll be your reckoning day."

"I'm looking forward to it." James frowned. "It's not like I'm going to be able to tell anyone while we're on the train."

Looking closer at the jewelry, he noticed one of the rings was missing its center, a crevice open where a stone surely had been. He put his forefinger through the thick ring band and brought it closer to his face. It looked like a collegiate ring, with engravings on either side. James could feel the lettering of the engravings on either side of the ring between the tips of his fingers, but whether the ring was a victim of the blood that stained the room, or the marking had faded away, he was unable to read the engravings. He wiped the ring on his pants.

"Use the curtain. Anything other than your clothes. Can you possibly fathom how hard it is to get blood out of clothes?"

James gave Martin a look before examining the ring. It was gold, with a small bident as one of the engravings. The other was one he hadn't seen before. It looked like a rounded maze with a six-pointed star in the middle. James stood in thought before placing the ring in his pocket. He looked down at the late Fiona Cross. He'd sworn to himself he would never get involved in something like this again, but then, it wasn't like he had a choice. James shook his head and mumbled something inaudible.

"Why would anyone hurt Fiona? She was such a sweet woman." Martin cleaned the front of his camera as he mused.

"Why does anyone hurt anyone?"

Martin smirked. "I can think of a couple of reasons."

"Do you have any decency? A woman was just murdered. This isn't the time to be making jokes."

"Someone has to lighten the mood."

"Lighten the mood? Not everything can be looked at through rose-colored glasses." James ran his hand through his hair, realizing too late that blood from the ring had stuck to his pale skin. He crinkled his nose.

Martin shrugged dismissively. "Who has anything to gain from her death?" He walked over to her vanity to pick at some of the jewelry.

"What were you doing up so late?" James raised an eyebrow.

"I have trouble falling asleep on trains." He shot James

a look, his eyes scanning him up and down. "I could ask you the same thing."

"That doesn't explain why you brought your camera."

"To take a picture of the coach at night while everyone is asleep. The quiet is sublime."

James pointed to the camera. "There is no way you can take a picture in such darkness."

"Well, it is a good thing I had it, now, isn't it?" Martin responded bitterly.

James realized he wasn't going to get anything more out of Martin, at least not tonight. "We need to know what happened and how she was killed. By her wounds, it looks like she was stabbed. So, who owns the weapon?" He thought, possible theories flashing before him.

"What happened? Let me see her!"

James and Martin heard a man's hoarse shout from the corridor and turned to the voice coming from that direction. Martin rushed to the doorway to block him.

Alexander appeared, his eyes glassy. His red tie was undone and hanging around his collar. Martin wrapped his arms around Alexander to hold him back.

"Get out of my way! That's my wife!" Alexander pushed against Martin as he attempted to move further into the room, which only made Martin tighten his hold.

Caught up in the struggle, it took a moment for Alexander's beet-red face to look up and notice James. He followed James's gaze to his wife's lifeless body. A wave of solemness shut him down; he closed his eyes and tightened his jaw. Noticing the change, Martin let go of Alexander, allowing him to slide down and sit on the carpet. He muttered a curse to himself.

"What is the meaning of all this?" Roger asked, his voice radiating from the hallway before he entered the room.

James looked past Roger to the young maid standing behind him, who looked captivated at the scene before realizing she wasn't alone in her thoughts. James refocused on the small man in front of him. "Can you come with me for a minute? I would like to—"

"We have to call the police," Roger insisted.

"We are on a moving train in the middle of nowhere," James said. "So, for right now, we need to find out what we can as soon as possible."

"And contaminate evidence?"

Martin saw the tension between the two men and interjected. "James is a part of the New York Police Department. He knows what he is doing."

"Thank you, Martin." James turned to Roger. "We need to stop at the closest station to investigate this case properly."

Alexander snorted as he stood back up from the carpet, pinching his shirt in place. "This is my train. I will be the one making those kinds of decisions. We are on a tight schedule, and I absolutely forbid stopping the train for your half-cocked investigation."

"What about your wife?"

"She is dead. She can wait." Alexander snorted. "Unless you want Chief Michaels to hear about this and get yourself fired, you will drop your request to stop any sooner than North Conway."

"I don't care if you get me fired, this is what's right."

"Playing the martyr, hmm? Well, if you don't care about what happens to you, then know that your investigation would ruin Michaels' reputation. And who would trust you after what you did anyway."

"You don't know anything about that," James whispered.

Alexander put his hand up. "No more investigating, or

I will throw you out to freeze to death in the snow. Am I clear?"

"Crystal," James said through clenched teeth. "Although, you do realize that if I'm not the one investigating, someone else will. The quicker we sort out the mess the quicker you will be able to continue with Elizabeth's tour."

"The tour? Why on Earth would this matter delay the tour?"

"Don't be dense," Martin began. "All members on board here will need to be at the ready for questioning at the station. Who knows how long that could last."

Roger stepped a couple of paces back from Alexander, whose frown deepened in the realization that he was outfoxed.

James looked between Alexander and Roger before adding. "At the very least, I'll be speaking to everyone on board about where they were tonight."

"Don't bother asking Alex," Roger said. "I can tell you now that he was probably off with that bearcat."

"She has a name, first of all, and I was not. I returned to my room a little after you retired, James." Alexander fixed his tie as he glanced at Roger.

"You know what you did," Roger spat.

"Now, now, little brother. This is neither the time nor the place." When no response was offered, Alexander smirked. "Good to see you do the respectable thing for once. Now, I am going to return to bed to rest up for this inquisition tomorrow." Alexander nodded collectively to the men before departing.

"Alexander, wait." James grimaced at the uncomfortable familiarity.

The man looked amused. "Already filled to the brim with questions?"

James ignored the comment. "Why are you and Fiona not sharing a compartment on your own train? Seems odd you would place yourself so far away from your spouse."

"She is the one who wanted it this way. She was very independent, and I simply didn't have the want or need to argue." He looked at Roger. "Had to let her win an argument every once in a while."

"Arguments? There were many?" James watched Roger flicker with irritation as Alexander turned to look back to where Fiona lay.

"She had a strong will. We had our differences, but nothing that amounted to this dreadful business."

James showed the brothers the ring missing its center. "Do either of you recognize this?"

"I can't say that I do." Roger responded first.

"Give it here," Alexander demanded. James hesitantly handed Alexander the ring. "Fiona has so many of the blasted things." He rotated the ring in the light. "It has been damaged, but still, I could sell it for its weight in gold." He put it in his pocket.

James held out his hand to Alexander. "We need the ring for evidence, but you will get it back when we figure this out."

Alexander sighed as he took the ring out of his pocket and handed it back to James. "Just because a ring is broken does not make it evidence."

"Well, we know it can't be Fiona's," Martin said.

The men turned to Martin, puzzled.

"I wrote about Fiona's allergy once when Elizabeth began working on her jewelry collection. Naturally, it was something that could be used to continue their rivalry." Martin shrugged. "Women love the gossip columns."

"Fiona was allergic to gold?" James asked.

Alexander shook his head. "Impossible. I know she wore gold, I certainly paid for it."

Martin relished in the reaction and took out his notebook, wanting to add more fuel to the fire.

"Now that you mention it, I don't think I've seen her wear gold recently," Roger said.

"Maybe it's a sudden change. Or it could very well be a lie," Martin added.

James walked over to where the other pieces of jewelry lay. "This is the only gold piece she brought. Why bring gold if she couldn't wear it? That is, if it was hers."

"It couldn't be hers. Trust me." Martin said.

James turned to look at Martin. "Whosever it is, we'll have to see who has a relationship with these symbols."

Roger looked to the window. "That's the problem with symbols; they can mean so many different things to people." He turned away from the men and tore down a green curtain to cover Fiona's body. James quietly took the opposing end. Together, they draped the cloth over her, making her look like a shrine of jade were it not for the blood that swam through the fabric.

Alexander pinched his lips together and sighed. "James, I'll be in my compartment when you want to see me."

James nodded, watching as Alexander walked over to his younger brother and placed a hand on his shoulder, squeezing it. He looked at Roger, then back at the curtain sprawled over his wife before leaving.

The uneasiness spread in the room like a disease. After another moment of silence, Martin moved toward James, the wood flooring squeaking underneath him. "Go easy on the man," Martin whispered in James's ear. "The magazines had a lot to say about these two."

James nodded, feeling a tug at his heart. He knew grief quite well.

"Fiona." The name came out as a whisper, almost inaudible. "Whoever did this, she never would have stood a chance." Roger's voice wavered. He grunted before straightening his back.

"Against what?" James asked cautiously.

"If someone came after her, she wouldn't have stood a chance. She couldn't hurt anyone, even if she knew they wanted to harm her."

"Who would want to hurt her?"

"Oh, no one. I'm speaking on her nature, her pure good will. She always did what was right. She was a North Star."

James shifted his weight, trying to not seem insensitive. He pushed down his feelings. "She seemed pretty upset while arguing with Clara tonight. Do you know what that was about?"

Roger sighed. "No, but she was always a wordsmith. Words were her preferred choice of weapon. Got her far, too." Roger solemnly looked toward the window, the sun starting to rise.

"A weapon she had to use often?" James asked.

Roger walked toward the compartment door. "I know you have a job to do, but can I get some sleep first? This is all very ... distressing." Roger looked possessed as he walked out without waiting for a response.

James was about to follow him when Martin put his arm in front of him. "Let him go, man, give them this night."

"We can't. You know how this works; we must start gathering alibis now before they have time to tighten or fabricate them."

"Everyone is asleep right now."

"Not everyone. We have a murderer on board."

"Or murderess. You need to get sleep to have a clear head for tomorrow. Trust me on that." Martin rubbed his eyes, the thought of sleep being quite agreeable. Seeing as James stood still, he continued. "What do you think of those two?"

James thought for a moment. "Roger and Alexander? They are the first people we will have to talk to. In terms of the crime scene, well, you see it just as well as I do."

"Someone should have heard something," Martin said.

"Perhaps. Then again, if this happened during the party, no one would have heard over the music."

Martin picked up Fiona's key, which rested on a small chestnut side table next to the door. "That porter said there was only one key per guest, meaning the only other person who could get in would be an employee."

James took the key from him. "Yes, unless Fiona left the door unlocked, then someone could've easily come upon her without the key in the first place." James picked at his cuticle.

"Jesus."

James nodded in agreement, holding up the ring. "At least we have somewhere to start."

"Well, you know where to find me if you need something." Martin yawned, stopping in the doorway on his way out to look back at James. "Promise me you won't continue this business till the morning."

James let out a weak smile. "You know I can't promise that."

After hearing Martin's footsteps fade down the corridor, he felt his eyelids grow heavy and decided to return to his room after all. He locked the door to Fiona's room and pocketed the key. It would have to suffice as securing the crime scene for the time being. James walked back to his own compartment slowly, letting sleep take over. After unlocking the door and walking inside, he almost slipped from something on the floor. "Shit," he whispered to himself, embarrassed at his carelessness. Catching himself on the frame of the door, he looked down to find that his foot had slid on a piece of paper. He picked it up and read the spiraling script on it.

## Maintenant, je ferai toujours partie de sa vie.

Now I will always be a part of her life.

James's brow furrowed in concentration as he took a seat on his makeshift bed, staring at the still partly wet blue ink that had transferred from the note onto his fingertips. He carefully placed the note in the copy of *Alice's Adventures in Wonderland*, while mentally thanking Anne for teaching him French all those years ago.

# Chapter Four

Light cascaded through the windows of James's compartment as the sun rose higher in the pale sky. Covering his face like a mask, the radiance made him squint as he pushed himself out of bed in response to a knock on his door. "One minute," he said, taking hold of the edges of his sheets to make his bed. He ran his fingers through the knots in his hair and looked at the small mirror on the wall to fix his cowlick. Noticing the small amount of ink stained on his hand from the note he received, memories of last night raced through his mind. Avoiding the ink, he rubbed his eyes and opened the door.

"Wow. It looks like you haven't slept in days."

"Good morning to you too, Martin. What do you want?"

"Just checking on you."

"How sweet," James responded. "Really, what is it?"

"We must get going on these interviews and start talking to people about last night. The press doesn't wait for anyone."

"We're not the press. I thought I made that clear to you."

Martin rolled his eyes. "I know when to include things or not."

James sighed. "Let's just get going."

"You're not going anywhere dressed like that." Martin looked James up and down, pointing out the bloodstains from last night on his pants and jacket. "Did you bring a change of clothes in that small suitcase of yours?"

James gave him a look before lifting his case from the silver rack and taking out a change of clothes. "I'll catch up with you."

"Don't be too long." Martin smiled, then headed toward the dining coach.

When James entered the dining coach, he was first drawn to the rectangular oak table in the middle, matching chairs with elegantly carved backpieces wrapped around it. On each chair, there was an emerald cushion with gold piping. Thin white linen laid over the table, with numerous spoons, forks, knives, and plates properly making up each place setting. At the head of the table sat Alexander, flanked by Elizabeth, Clara, and Roger. The coach's velvet green curtains were tied back with thick golden ropes, which allowed for the two horizontal windows on each side to let the morning sun reflect against the crystal glasses on the table.

Alexander caught sight of James. "Mr. Anderson, would you join the rest of us for breakfast? The maid has prepared a lovely meal for us. Did she not, Elizabeth?"

Elizabeth looked up. "Why, of course."

James pulled out a chair and took a seat at the opposing head of the table.

"Now, on to business." Alexander straightened in his seat, fixing the collar of his shirt before continuing. "James, I've spoken to my brother, and in the best interests of everyone here, we wish no further investigation into the death of my poor wife, God bless her."

James squirmed in his chair. "I want to be respectful, but you can't stop this investigation. I will share what I said to you and your brother with everyone here. If it is not me conducting this case, then another officer will investigate it once we reach the station," James said matter-of-factly. He noticed Elizabeth dart her eyes from him to Alexander.

Martin spoke up. "Fiona would want us to figure out what happened. She didn't deserve to be stabbed in such a grotesque fashion."

There was a gasp at the table. Clara's face turned white.

"Stabbed?" Elizabeth repeated.

James shot Martin a menacing look.

"They're her family. They have the right to know."

James sighed before resting his forehead between his thumb and forefinger.

Elizabeth spoke up. "A woman does not want her life or body to be examined by the likes of you or any man. It's quite unnatural in death."

"If you want to find out what happened to her, she needs to be examined professionally," James replied calmly, having had this conversation on other cases.

"She doesn't need to be examined at all. She was murdered. Isn't that enough?" Elizabeth said, hitting her gloved hand against the table for emphasis.

As Elizabeth closed her eyes to steady herself, James noticed Dean emerge from the hallway.

"Would you like a drink, Miss Kingston?" Dean asked, as if on cue.

"I'll have another Mon Coeur Tea with lemon, Dean, darling. You know what I like." Elizabeth smiled, completely recomposed.

"Your usual. Of course, miss." Dean responded as he picked up her cup from the table.

"What a good lad," Clara mumbled as she poured herself a cup of coffee.

James picked up the conversation. "The way we found her body and the surrounding scene will help us figure out who committed the act and why. A pathologist looking after her body will help us learn what happened."

"We will figure this out," Martin said. "There is no reason to worry."

"Playing detective will only get you in trouble," Roger said, causing Martin's face to flush a deep red.

Elizabeth looked at Martin. "Oh, now don't be embarrassed," she said. "Let's be honest, you of all people aren't the best at understanding women. From what I read in the *Times*, your wife—"

Martin stood abruptly, causing his chair to fall back behind him. "Don't you dare say anything against my wife! I don't care that you're a woman, you will be under my hand if you say another word."

"So it was true. Very interesting," Elizabeth said.

"Let's not get feisty." Clara stood, clutching a small pink purse with golden tassels. It had a delicate design, with two parallel spirals with peacocks on either side of the bag. "Now, to the matter at hand. No more investigation from you boys. I don't want you to be associated with this mess. Martin, you may be familiar with the dark side of the press, but James..." She frowned, her eyes pleading before feeling for her seat and sitting back down.

"An excellent point, Clara," Alexander said. "James, our family and its associations will keep you in the limelight for a while if you continue. Why not wait until we get to North Conway?"

"We have no time to lose. This isn't something that is up for debate," James said.

The door from the kitchen swung open and Dean emerged with Elizabeth's Mon Coeur tea, a white drip towel swaying over his forearm. Elizabeth smiled as she received the tea and thanked him, watching as he closed the kitchen door as he left.

"I agree with James." It was a meek response from Roger, who kept his eyes on his silverware.

Elizabeth stood up and slammed down her cup on the saucer. "What utter nonsense! You're blind with grief."

"Now wait a moment, Elizabeth. We can't let ourselves get too emotional." Alexander curled his fingers around his spoon, tapping at the hard-boiled egg in front of him.

"Since there seems to be no relenting of your stubbornness. I offer you this. You may do your little investigation, but under two conditions. You will not touch my dear wife's body, and under no circumstances are we stopping until we get to North Conway. Got it?"

James shrugged, "That is a good start."

Elizabeth's eyes darkened as she turned to Alexander, then stormed out of the room. Alexander nodded to Roger before following her.

"What was that about?" James asked, glancing between Roger, Clara, and Martin as he tried to read their faces.

"She's a celebrity. She won't have it if the attention is not on her all the time," Roger said with a sneer, having regained his confidence.

"Take it easy, Roger. She's going through her own issues," Clara said.

"Aren't we all? She wants to upstage Fiona even when she's been murdered." Roger clenched his fists on the table. He shook his head. "I better check the damage."

Clara watched him leave, absentmindedly fingering a silver chain around her neck that held a ruby pendant.

"What an interesting necklace you have there, Clara. Where did you get it?" James asked.

"From a little store in North Conway I visited with my daughter during the summer. I'll be sure to return with your compliment."

"You have a daughter?"

Clara smiled. "Seems the most unlikely people are the ones stuck with children, hmm?" She touched her neck gracefully, toying with the chain. The necklace was embedded with two small diamonds on either side of the glaring ruby in the middle. A small ruby ring glittered against the soft wrinkles on her hand.

"Rubies are alright, I suppose. Emeralds are my stone of choice. Fiona got me an emerald makeup mirror for my birthday last May. That shimmering lush green, there's nothing like it. I got her a ruby ring for her birthday last month; she always had an affinity for rubies. They're not really in this season, but I'd do anything for Fiona. I asked Elizabeth if I could borrow this little ruby ring for Fiona when I found out this morning that she passed," Clara said sheepishly.

"What are you doing for Fiona?"

"Honoring her, James. You're a man, so you wouldn't understand how these little symbols can mean so much to a woman of our stature."

Martin picked up his coffee cup. "Do you often wear symbols?"

"Here and there. I love Victorian jewelry and the rich symbolism of it. Not that I can afford it."

Martin humored her. "What kind of symbols are there?"

"Goodness what a question. There must be hundreds of symbols to know and use. You have to keep in mind that during the Victorian period there was a strict etiquette of how one portrayed themselves to the world, and women took pride in their symbols because of that. Jewelry is a way to express our identity and beliefs, with each design having its own meaning, which could also describe the owner. Queen Victoria's engagement ring from Prince Albert with the snake motif is one of the most widely known."

"An engagement ring with a snake? Why a snake?" Martin asked. "That seems to go against other cultural representations of snakes."

"Snakes symbolized eternity, wisdom, and everlasting love in the Victorian era. Therefore, when someone was to see Queen Victoria's ring, it would mean the prince and queen had a smart marriage that would last forever with lots of love."

"But that wasn't the only well-known symbol at the time," James stated.

Clara turned to him. "Definitely not. Birds like owls, swallows, and doves were popular, representing wisdom, vigilance, motherhood, and peace in some cases. Then you have insects, like the butterfly that was a symbol for the soul, or dragonflies who represented prosperity, courage, and change. Clover and horseshoes for good fortune, hands like those on claddagh rings in Ireland. Then there are birth months, for example I was born in May so I may wear a lily of the valley which represents motherhood, sweetness, or hope. I could go on and on, and that's not even mentioning lockets, acrostic, and mourning jewelry."

"What about a bident? What did that symbolize in the Victorian era?" James asked.

Clara shook her head. "I am by no means an expert, but I haven't heard of any specific meaning for a bident. However, thinking about astronomy, the crescent moon and stars were popular symbols and motifs. Like the North Star, stars symbolized direction. Think about it like how sailors would look to the stars to guide them through the dark nights at sea. Stars also were used to represent the spirit but were often worn with a crescent moon. The crescent moon symbol originates from the ancient times and the spiritual powers of different deities. Then, of course, there is Greek or Roman mythology in relation to the moon goddesses Artemis or Diana, whichever you prefer, as well as Hecate. Womanhood and female empowerment were celebrated by women through the crescent-like jewelry. It also sometimes showed a desire for a new relationship or marriage since the moon is constantly phasing." Clara clasped her hands together and blushed. "Oh, I am very sorry for my rambling. My mother always spoke of symbolism and Victorian jewelry."

"That's quite alright." James said, looking over to find Martin letting out a yawn. "Speaking of symbolism, why are you wearing rubies for Fiona?"

"I've known Fiona my entire life. She was wrapped up in a lot of problems that were not her own, but she was such a strong woman. Red is a strong color, and we must all be brave. For her sake."

James watched as she twirled the ring around her finger.

Martin pushed away from the table. "I'm going back to my compartment. Get me if you need anything," he said, then left.

Clara leaned toward James. "While we are here

together, just the two of us, what are your thoughts on Fiona's … circumstance? This type of thing, it's just not done. I'm worried for you." Clara's hand shook as she picked up her ceramic cup and brought it to her lips.

James reached for her other hand across the table. "We'll be fine, don't worry about us."

Clara pulled her hand back.

"Do you know anyone who would have wanted to harm Fiona for any reason?" James asked softly.

Clara slowly returned the cup to its saucer. "Fiona was loved by everyone. No, you'd better look at the Cross family itself." Clara looked around to make sure they were alone before gesturing for him to lean in. "They had a lot of enemies, even among themselves. I worked for them for a time."

"In what capacity?"

"A lady's maid. I originally worked for Fiona's mother. Once Fiona was married, I followed her to the Cross estate."

"How was working for her mother and the Cross estate."

"Working for Fiona's mother was the best four years of my life. No one would take me in since I didn't have any references, but her mother gave me a chance as a scullery maid, and I worked my way up. Fiona was my best friend, and I would have done anything for her."

"I couldn't help but overhear the other day that you two were arguing. What was it about?"

"That's all very complicated, and not an appropriate conversation for the morning." Clara let out a weak smile. "Come, have some coffee. Or is tea more fitting?"

"Coffee is better, it keeps me awake." James smiled.

"It must have been hard for you to sleep last night?"

"It has come to be hard for me to sleep any night."

James took the pot of coffee from the table and poured some into his cup.

"This circumstance won't make it any easier for you, but what is life without a challenge?" Clara asked.

"I'm hoping it'll make me exhausted, so that I can't help but fall asleep." James chuckled, smelling the comforting aroma of coffee.

Clara's thin lips raised into a smile as they touched the edge of her cup, turning solemn upon hearing Elizabeth's stiletto heels hit the polished wood flooring of the dining room.

"Is Clara bothering you with her stories again?" Elizabeth laughed, perching her hands on the back of a dining chair.

James put down his coffee. "On the contrary, it has been quite interesting."

Elizabeth scoffed. "No need to be polite. Come, Roger is waiting to talk to you."

"Well, I would've thought more of him if he had asked to talk to me himself. It's not like I'm difficult to find," James jested, waiting for a reaction.

"No, you're quite easy to find. But I don't think that is always a good thing. Especially for you." Elizabeth took her gloved hands off the chair and started back the way she came.

"You can tell him I'll be there in a minute," James said.

She was at the end of the compartment when the rhythmic clicks of her shoes stopped. She flicked her hair back as she spun to look at James. "I'm not a messenger. If you want to speak with him, be a man and address him yourself." She looked to Clara, then forced a smile on her blood-red lips. "You better be there soon. He doesn't like waiting." She raised a brow tauntingly, the irony seemed to be lost on her that she was acting as messenger for Roger.

Her dress swished across her knees as she strode into the next compartment.

Clara cleared her throat. "It's young fools like you who get hurt in these shenanigans."

James shrugged as his eyes met Clara's. "I'll be alright. If words hurt, I'd already be dead."

He smiled, but that only made Clara shake her head.

James decided, in spite, that Roger could wait a few more minutes. Instead, he went to speak to Martin about the film from last night. When James reached 6A, he knocked three times. On the third knock, Martin opened the door. He had rolled up his white sleeves and had a pencil tucked behind his left ear.

"What do you need? I'm kind of in the middle of something right now."

"Do you have the film from the other night? Perhaps we can find somewhere safe to store it until we get to North Conway."

"About that." Martin took the pencil from behind his ear and twirled it in his fingers. "The film got exposed to light, it's ruined."

"How is that possible? You took it just last night. It should still be in your camera."

"I don't know what happened. I came back from breakfast to find the film lying out across my desk." Martin pointed back to his camera underneath the window, the film ripped out of the box and exposed in the sun.

"Who would want to destroy it?" James wondered aloud.

"I usually leave my room unlocked, so anyone could've come in."

"The only people who saw you with your camera last night were Roger and Alexander," James said, his eyes examining the yellow walls in the compartment as he reflected on the previous evening.

"What would they get from destroying my film?" Martin shrugged as he sat on the makeshift couch behind the desk.

"I have a couple of ideas, but forgive me for saying, you don't seem very upset that this happened."

A small fire grew in Martin's eyes. "Those were the cat's meow. Front page worthy. Now, I must settle for some sunset or the White Mountains like every other sap. I'm not upset, I'm furious. You should have been here when I first found it like this. I've had some time to accept it is all."

"At least they didn't break your camera," James said, leaning against the doorway.

Martin sighed. "That would've been easier for them. Not everyone knows how to work with film." Martin threw the ruined film into the garbage. "Although, yes, I'm glad they didn't break it. That wouldn't be a good start to the day, not like this is any better."

"I imagine it wouldn't be." James glanced down the hallway and sighed when he saw Roger looking for him.

Roger's frown deepened when he saw James. "So, this is where you are. I thought you were coming to see me."

"I was just on my way."

"I don't like my time being wasted. I won't stand for it."

James rolled his eyes. "If you wanted to speak to me, you should've found me yourself. We're not all your playthings."

"Listen, you. I stuck my neck out for you to continue your silly little investigation. You will adhere to me."

"Onward then, you have me now," he said sarcastically.

Satisfied with the response, Roger escorted James down the hallway and into the heart of the train. At the door of Roger's compartment, Roger put out his hand nonchalantly for James to go in first, promptly following behind him and closing the door. Roger's compartment was roughly the same size as Fiona's. A pale blue paint livened up the otherwise dark, gothic woodwork seen in the craftsmanship of the furniture about the room.

"Take a seat. I'll pour you a glass of my finest red before we discuss business." Roger directed James to one of the blue-cushioned chairs before reaching for a bottle from his spirits cart. "You see, I'm a very private man. I don't need to know your affairs as much as you need to know mine." He steadied two glasses on the tray and poured.

"I understand that, sir, but these are unusual circumstances and anything you can tell me could be helpful in figuring out who would want to—"

"There are a few things you ought to understand. First, I am only telling you this for Fiona's sake. I know you have to speak to me eventually, and I'd rather you hear my piece before you hear Alexander's." Roger sipped his glass before walking to his chair and placing the drink in front of James.

"I will evaluate everyone's accounts fairly regardless of the time they're given," James replied. "Where were you last night?"

Roger sighed as he fell into the chair opposing James. "Alex and I were in this room discussing our mother's estate. We needed to go through her will and sell the house."

"I heard that the William A. Clark House is being sold.

It is a shame." James picked at a hangnail while they conversed.

"Yes, well our mother lived in an estate of that nature, and in these times, it costs a fortune to sustain."

"I can imagine. Where does your mother live?"

"Lenox, Massachusetts. But we are taking our train through North Conway on a vacation before going south to secure the selling of the estate. Then there is Elizabeth's tour, of course."

James took a sip of his wine and grimaced, then set it on the table. "Fiona was your sister-in-law?"

Roger chuckled at James's expression. "You clearly have never tasted fine wine before. Yes. Fiona married my brother twenty-two long years ago."

"Was she a good fit in the family?"

"Of course she was." Roger's face softened as he glanced out the window. "In every way," he added, pulling both sides of his jacket together.

"Did she have any enemies you can think of?"

"She was a lovely woman, always able to see the good in people. Even my brother. Look, Mr. Anderson—" Roger pulled out his checkbook from a pocket inside his jacket.

James sighed. "What are you doing?"

"You seem like a decent man who wants the best for Fiona. What she would want is for you to forget about this. Give up on this before you can't get out." Roger placed the check between them.

James shook his head and folded his hands. "I can't accept this. Your money doesn't put you above the law. Why did you stand up for me to keep investigating a few hours ago only to shut it down now?"

"Oh, come on. I'm sure you need the money. It can be our little secret." Roger smiled presumptuously.

"I'm sorry, but figuring out why her life was taken is more important to me."

"You think it's not important to me?" Roger stood, astounded.

James stood as well and adjusted his jacket. "She was murdered. We have to do what we can for her by figuring out who did this. Don't you understand?" James paused for a moment and then sat down. "Homicides always occur for a reason. Wealth, jealousy, revenge."

"Why would anyone hurt her? Who would dare do such a thing?" Roger retook his seat and dropped his head into his hands.

James relaxed his shoulders. "I'm sorry for your loss, Roger. It's not easy to—"

"Don't take me for one of 'em pansies. If you won't accept my money, then ask me what you will. Let's get this damn thing over with."

"Did Alexander and Fiona have a happy marriage?" James asked. He watched Roger's eyes dance around the room.

"You could say they did, but even a 'happy marriage' isn't always smooth sailing." Roger took a watch out of his jacket. "Are you married, Mr. Anderson?"

"I, well, it's complicated," James replied.

"Well, there are a lot of parts in a marriage, things someone like you wouldn't understand." Roger let a bitter smile tug at the corner of his mouth.

James spoke through his teeth. "This isn't about me."

"Struck a nerve there, did I?" Roger laughed, returning James's stare with distaste before looking out the window. "Listen, I loved my sister-in-law, and I wished her no ill will. What she got herself involved in is beyond me."

James stood and walked around the compartment,

taking in the blue composition of the room. He walked by Roger's desk, noticing a small stack of business cards.

"Alexander brought up concern about the upkeep of the train. That must be upsetting," James said.

"It does cost my brother a small fortune to run, but he prefers to keep the legacy going. Our father was the same, always stuck in his old ways. I suppose that's where he got it from."

"How long has the train been in your family's possession?"

"Who knows."

"Alexander said you were a train enthusiast."

Roger smirked. "Did he? So that's what silly excuse he used."

"Used for what?"

"The train was supposed to be sold years ago; we had a high offer, but Alexander refused. Him and his stubborn pride." Roger held out his arms. "All of this is just one charade after the other. I know he wants to preserve our high class and legacy, but what does that really mean. We're in the red."

"What have you been doing to get yourselves out of it?" James asked.

Roger shrugged. "Making cash here and there. It's gotten better recently. But with bigger debts, you must take bigger risks."

"What debts have you had to deal with?"

"Let me show you. You'd find out soon enough." Roger placed his wine glass on the table and lumbered over to his desk. He pulled out the top drawer, his stubby fingers plucking through colored folders. Finding the first two folders empty, Roger dropped them to the side and picked up the one that resided at the bottom of the pack. He weighed the folder in his hands and sighed. "Here she is."

Roger handed the folder to James and took a step back, as if something would jump out of the pages.

James used both hands as he grasped the thick folder, being careful to not let the documents slip out. The folder was navy, its silver threaded spine ripped from heavy use. James opened the folder and picked through the first few documents, scanning through the numbers and reports. His eyes widened as he peeled the thin documents apart and found a log of five, thousand-dollar withdrawals written to 'Moon Swallow' from only a couple of days ago.

"Who's Moon Swallow?" James asked. He looked to the right of the page, looking for Roger's signature, but the panel was blank. "And why haven't you signed it?"

"I never sign, I send my business card instead." Roger replied.

"And Moon Swallow?"

"I don't know who it is," Roger stated.

"Why are you paying them?"

"I owe a large gambling debt. They've been gracious enough to let me pay it in part each month."

"I'm not sure if 'gracious' is the word I would use in this case," James said, thoughtful. He plucked one of the business cards from the desk, feeling the sharp edges of the maroon card between his fingers as he studied the stiff silver lettering. Roger's name glittered in the middle, above an address and phone number. James flipped it over to find a script letter H on top of a bident. James pocketed the card.

"This process would go a lot faster if you told me the truth." James took out the gold ring that was found in Fiona's compartment, tracing the stamped lines of the bident. "Is this your ring?"

"I've been completely upfront about everything, don't accuse me of lying."

"Just answer the question. Is this yours?" James positioned the ring in front of Roger.

"No, it's far too small for me." Roger showed his hand. "My finger would never fit through the—" He cut himself off and squinted at the ring. "Can I see that for a moment?"

James handed him the ring. Roger weighed it in his hand before feeling the engravings.

"I thought I lost this ring years ago."

"You recognize it?"

"Yes." Roger twirled it in the light. "But it looks different now. You see this engraving here?" He pointed a finger toward the maze. "This is new. I don't recognize the symbol. And the gemstone is missing."

James shook his head. "So you're saying someone resized it and added the carving?"

"I know it doesn't make any sense, but yes. The ring originally held a gemstone beside a bident. I'm flabbergasted that it was found in Fiona's things."

James was pensive for a moment. "What does the bident mean to you?"

"It's from Greek mythology. The bident was a weapon associated with Hades, or Pluto, the ruler of the underworld."

"What about Hades made you wear the symbol? Isn't Hades considered evil in some context?"

"People have always feared death. Naturally then, they would fear the God of Death. Let me make this clear though; Hades might be depicted as evil in modern times, but he was fair and respected. That is what I strive for." Roger put the file back into the top drawer and closed it. He then put his hand on James's back. "I think that is enough for now. I won't take up more of your time."

"Our time here has given me a lot to think about."

James walked with Roger to the door and stood in the corridor.

"I'm sure it has." Roger leaned against the doorway, hesitant to continue. "I won't lie to you though; I don't wish to do this again."

When the door closed in his face, James flinched and took a step back, walking into the dainty tea cart of the young maid. Jams, biscuits, and little cakes hit the gold and red carpeted floor, followed by a shower of forks, spoons, and knives.

"I'm so sorry," James said, tugging up the fabric of his pants as he crouched to the ground to pick up what had fallen.

"It's nothing to worry about, sir," she responded, bending over to help.

James stood up with the silverware he'd collected and handed it to her. "Call me James, if you don't mind. And you are?" he asked, brushing off his pants.

"Ruth Crownley, but never refer to me by my surname. It's Ruth to you. Now, do you mind?" She motioned toward Roger's door, which James was blocking.

"I'm sorry."

"You apologize too much." Ruth smirked, then walked into Roger's compartment.

Shaking his head, James walked back toward the dining car, hoping some water would help lessen the redness he felt bloom across his face.

# Chapter Five

James loosened his shoulders while he poured himself a drink. The window above the bar acted like a moving portrait of the vast lush green trees and hills in the distance. He opened the window and closed his eyes, the fresh air reinvigorating him.

Martin strode in, a different colored pencil behind his ear, and closed the window. "What'd'ya think you're doing? Look at you lollygagging when we have a crime to solve."

"I'm working on it," James muttered. "Where have you been?"

"I've been here and there, listening, observing. People tend not to notice me."

James raised an eyebrow and chuckled. "I find that highly unlikely. At least, I'd notice a face like yours anywhere."

"Very funny. I'm dying laughing over here." Martin rolled his eyes.

"It sounds as if I'm interrupting something," said Alexander as he approached the bar. His formal manner created a coolness in the room.

"I'm glad you're here," James said. "I was hoping you could answer some questions."

Alexander raised his brow. "It seems like that's all I've been doing lately."

James gestured toward a chair. "Who has been asking questions?"

"Oh, everyone. Wanting to know what I thought about Fiona." Alexander pulled out the chair to take a seat. "I do hope lunch will be served soon. Our cook knows I don't like to be kept waiting."

Martin followed suit and pulled out a chair of his own. "I would've expected you to be in the company of Elizabeth."

"She is very much capable of fending for herself, Mr. O'Reilly. She's not my dog."

"I didn't mean to insult," Martin forced himself to say.

"Then you're doing a rather poor job expressing yourself. I expected better from a writer. That is what you do, isn't it?" Alexander placed his napkin across his lap and then grasped the menu laid out in front of him.

"Did you think Fiona needed tending after?" James asked. He felt two pairs of eyes latch on him as he pulled out a seat next to Martin.

"My wife was a different breed of woman, one with class, elegance, and a way with words. A lady such as that needs protection from the brutality of the world. If only from societal expectations. She was my partner, and while we didn't always see eye to eye, we were faithful to one another. We made a vow in front of God, and I would never do anything to break it."

Alexander shifted his position, turning to Martin.

"Whatever I say will not be printed or you will hear from my lawyers." Alexander's voice was like a wave as it grew in volume. "Society is cold and cruel, and I want none of our affairs printed."

Martin shrugged. "I can't promise anything. And if you have nothing to hide, then there is nothing to be afraid of."

Alexander showed his perfect white teeth. "There is nothing wrong with a little privacy. And do you need a reminder that you are my guest, eating my food, at my table."

Dean walked across the golden carpet, dressed head to toe in his uniform. He stopped at the table and waited for instruction. James properly looked over the man. His dark hair was swept to the side with a few strands in front of his eyes. His face was solemn, like a china doll dressed as an exhibit of wealth and decoration.

Alexander threw out a smile. "I will have the clam bisque and creamed mushrooms, Mr. Bradley. Thank you."

Dean turned to Martin expectantly, revealing a small scar behind his ear.

"I will have the jellied chicken. Make that two servings. I know James hasn't eaten anything."

James grimaced.

Dean collected the menus without a word and walked to the kitchen. Soon, he returned with a water pitcher, meticulously leaning over to pour the same amount of liquid into each glass. The men sat in silence, only hearing the faint trickling from the water pitcher into the glasses. Dean left the room as quietly as he had entered.

"You're not wearing your wedding ring?" James asked, noticing Alexander's hand as he picked up his glass.

Alexander parted the glass from his lips. "Very observant. I take it off so I don't lose it. That way, I know where it is and have peace of mind."

James took the napkin before him and placed it on his

lap. "Wouldn't it give you more comfort if it rested on your finger?"

"Perhaps, for some. It was a gift from Fiona's father before we were wed." Alexander took a deep breath and leaned back in his chair. "I know enough about these investigations to know you two are here to pin her death on me. I'm sure others have indicated I was responsible."

"We are not suggesting you did anything, Mr. Cross. But we do have to figure out what we can. So please excuse me when I ask, where were you last night?" James watched as Alexander shifted his weight in the chair.

Alexander covered his mouth in thought at first. "I was at the party and had a couple of drinks, then Lizzy and I walked to the terrace off the back to smoke for a bit. After that, I went to see my brother to go over our mother's estate."

"You and Elizabeth must be close." James heard scratching and looked over to see Martin writing in his notebook under the table. If Alexander noticed, he didn't say anything.

"You become close when working in our world," said Alexander. "She has a beautiful voice. I'm only doing my job to help her reach her full potential. She has the talent and I have the contacts."

Dean entered the coach and placed the men's meals before them.

James picked up his fork and prodded the jellied chicken, which jiggled in return. "Did Fiona show any concerns about Elizabeth? She must've taken up a lot of your time."

Alexander closed his eyes and wafted the rich aroma of clam bisque and creamed mushrooms with his hand. He didn't answer for a moment, then slowly opened his eyes to reach for a spoon. "I told Fiona everything. She deserved that at least. If she trusted me as much as I trusted her, then she had nothing to worry about." He delicately placed his spoon into the bowl and blew on the steam rising from the dish.

"How much did you trust her?" James took a bite and swallowed, forcing down the meal he had before him.

"I trusted her with my life, not that it matters now."

The rest of lunch was quiet as the three men went about eating their meals. Alexander was the first to be done, promptly pushing in his chair and striding away. Martin and James walked back to their compartments, agreeing to reconvene later in the day to discuss the investigation.

When James reached his room, he used his key to open the door. Instead of the bed that he had made earlier, Dean had folded it back into a couch. James fell onto the small couch and leaned his head against the wall. After a moment, he took off his jacket and rolled up the sleeves of his white button-down shirt.

Clara's shrill voice rang like a parakeet as her heavy steps marched down the carpeted hallway of the train car. "James! Oh, where is that boy?"

Reluctantly, James opened the door of his compartment. "What's wrong, Clara?"

"Oh, James, I knew you were here." She pushed her hair behind her ears.

"Where else would I be?"

Clara put her index finger to her lips to silence him. "I do not need that tone. I need to speak to you. Immediately," she snapped, anger sweeping over her face faster than the wind.

"Alright, relax." James stepped into the hallway and motioned for Clara to come in and take a seat on the couch. He followed her inside and closed the compartment door. Clara straightened the skirt of her black dress as she sat down. James sat on the opposing side of the couch.

"First of all, never tell a woman to relax. It has exactly the opposite effect." She raised her brow. "Now, I know Fiona was stabbed, but as for the weapon, she was killed with a letter opener, wasn't she?" Clara sat motionlessly.

James was quiet, letting Clara fill the silence.

"My letter opener was stolen, so I know what was done to her." Clara tightened her pale lips.

James reevaluated Clara, who rolled out her neck like a snake as she relished in her presumed knowledge of the murder weapon.

"If you have come to me for nothing more than answers to your own inquiry—"

Clara's back stiffened as she raised her nose. "I suppose a man of your stature couldn't tell the difference between what is valuable or not." Clara crinkled her nose as she looked around his room.

"I'd like to think I know enough. Starting with the fact the value of a trivial object, such as a letter opener, is of less importance than the woman who may have been slain by it."

"I'll have you know this was an ornate silver letter opener that was handmade in France, with rubies from the Kingdom of Fife in Scotland."

"If that brings you joy, who am I to judge?" James watched her hands unclench and grasp for the fabric of her skirt.

"You're a policeman and I command you to take this seriously."

James raised his brow incredulously. "You command me?"

"Well, if you're not going to be professional about it,

then I will. I have reason to believe Elizabeth took it. And if you do not—"

James put his hands up in defense. "Listen, Clara, I will file a police report for you when we get to North Conway. But for the time being—"

"That's more like it. But I will be reporting this to your superior." She pushed her hair behind her shoulders.

"It won't be anything he hasn't heard already. But I'm curious, why would Elizabeth take your letter opener? Surely, she could buy one herself."

Clara's demeanor softened. "My letter opener was a one of a kind. I saw her eyeing it when we first got on board. I think she had more sinister reasons for wanting it." Clara paused. "I will ask again, and this time I hope you have an answer. Fiona was murdered with this letter opener, was she not? I must confirm."

"Clara, I am a policeman, as you say," James replied. "So don't you trifle with the matters of this investigation."

Clara smiled an unseemly smile and leaned back against the wall as she made herself more comfortable. "We were close friends, Mrs. Cross and I, but you wouldn't have known that from the other night. I will have to live with the fact that was our last conversation."

"What were you arguing about?" James folded his hands in his lap.

"Roger wanted Elizabeth to help him launch his new business."

"I don't understand. That doesn't concern either of you."

She muttered something inaudible under her breath. "It concerns us just as much as this case concerns you," Clara snapped before pausing to calm herself down. "Fiona had discovered Elizabeth was given an allowance for helping Roger. She wasn't pleased about it."

"An allowance? Why?"

"Elizabeth asked him for money to help her make a jewelry collection."

"But she's famous. I'm sure a lot of different companies would be thrilled to work with her. Even so, I don't see how this connects to you."

"I was standing up for Elizabeth. The Cross family has a lot of money, and if Elizabeth needed some what was the issue? She's the one making Alexander rich on top of his family fortune."

"I feel like I'm missing something. If Elizabeth already has a lot of money, why is it she can't afford to work with a jewelry company, so much so she has to borrow money from her manager's brother? Why didn't Fiona want to give her the money?" James scratched his head.

"Even celebrities can run up debt, or God knows what she is into. I don't know why she needed the money to come from him. Not like it matters now."

James was contemplative as he leaned back against the wood, mirroring Clara's posture. "Alexander must spend a lot of time with Elizabeth. More than time home with Fiona?"

"Elizabeth works for Alexander. He is the reason she is where she is today. Fiona said she rarely saw him lately, but she was a beautiful woman and men were never too far behind to scoop her up."

"Did Fiona have reason to believe Alexander had more than a working relationship with Elizabeth?" James watched as Clara looked down at her hands.

"Oh, you're talking nonsense. Alexander is the most conservative man you will ever meet. Believe me, I know. Even after his mother died, he continued all her old ways." She paused to look back up at James. "Besides, just because he has to make public appearances with

Elizabeth does not mean he is having an affair with her. That's just the press trying to sell papers. You can ask your friend Martin all about that. The press can be terrible."

"Did Mrs. Cross have a happy marriage?" James refocused the conversation.

"They had a trying relationship."

"Because of Miss Kingston?"

Clara sighed. "Who can say what goes on behind closed curtains and locked doors. She always had Roger, the spare. I never could figure out what either man wanted, so I doubt anyone knew."

James tilted his head. "And what is it that you want?"

"An opportunity to do something with my life in a world that already has such strict limitations on the capabilities of women. Is that all your questions? I feel rather tired and might need a cup of tea."

"I was wondering—"

"Here we go," Clara cut him off bitterly.

"You mentioned earlier about Victorian symbolism— snakes, insects, moons, birds."

"What of it?" Clara swatted the air with her hand, pushing away the moment.

"What would it mean to have a moon and a swallow together?"

Clara's eyes narrowed like a hawk's. "Why?"

James shrugged. "Just curious. Our conversation inspired me. It's nice hearing what people are passionate about."

Clara's face reddened. "I can't be certain, but the significance may come from the combination of the symbols. Perhaps you would have better luck looking at older jewelry pieces with different symbolisms. Maybe this relates to a piece of jewelry Fiona had that Alexander purchased for her, but I don't think Alexander would be aware of Victorian symbols."

"And if he was aware of the symbols," James pressed.

Clara looked out the window. "The swallow or dove was commonly handed to brides to be from their fiancé to count as the 'something new' portion of the old rhyme. You know: something old, something new, something borrowed, something blue. Specifically, the husband would buy a piece of jewelry with a swallow because swallows mate for life and always go back to their nest. This made it a popular symbol for motherhood." Clara put her hand to her chin in thought. "The combination of both a swallow and a moon makes it a very feminine symbol, regardless. It doesn't suit Alexander now, does it? Not his style."

"I suppose not. I found some documents that had the name Moon Swallow on them. It was on a payroll, perhaps. Do you know who might refer to themselves as Moon Swallow?"

Her eyes widened in alarm. "What documents?"

"They were on Fiona's desk," James lied. "Do you know a Moon Swallow?" he asked again.

Clara raised her hands "My goodness, no. That's far too vague. I'm sure there are scores of people who could go by that."

"But you are a suspect with previous knowledge on these symbols and their meanings. Are you Moon Swallow? Were you receiving money from Mr. Cross or any member of the family?"

"Like I would take money from those brothers. Their money is filthy. I have always been invested in hard work. Hard work and determination created the woman you see today."

"Money is still money. You know everything about

them, perhaps there is something you know they don't want me to know. What was Mr. Cross paying you for?"

"Enough! I have been telling you everything I know and answering your little questions. I don't plan on telling you anything more about my private business."

"Then, if you don't mind me asking an easy one, where were you when Mrs. Cross was murdered?"

Clara seethed before answering. "I was in my coach sleeping, although I don't get much of that these days." She pulled out a small emerald mirror from her purse to fix her makeup. "Speaking of sleep, if you are done with your unsettling questions, I think I'm going to get some rest." Without waiting for an answer, she stood up and flattened her skirt to leave.

"Thank you," James said, standing up after her.

Clara scoffed. "Don't forget about that police report. I expect to get my letter opener as soon as possible. This also doesn't change anything; I will be writing to your superior."

"I wouldn't have it any other way." James shook his head, hiding a faint smile as Clara left.

Once she was gone, James sat down on the bench and leaned his back against the window. He tried to fall asleep, but thoughts whirled through his mind as the puzzle pieces kept shifting. He wiped his eyes with the back of his hand, then looked himself over in the small mirror on the wall. Red blood vessels from restless nights ornamented the whites of his eyes.

Even when he could fall asleep, the only thing he could see was Anne. Her pale body lifeless as she laid on the cuff of the lake, the water pushing her hair back. Every nightmare was the same—drowning in the sand as he ran toward her, every time hoping he would be able to save her this time.

# Chapter Six

James decided the best way to clear his head would be to go for a walk. He had only gone a couple of paces when he noticed the door of the women's bathroom swinging open at the end of the hall. At the sound of a large crash, he hurried his pace and watched as cosmetics rolled out of the small bathroom. Ruth stepped out to pick up the items and jumped when she saw James.

"You scared the living daylights out of me," she said in an accusatory tone, putting one hand over her heart.

"I'm sorry, I didn't mean to scare you," James replied, color growing on his cheeks.

Ruth tucked a loose strand of hair behind her ear before falling to her knees to collect the various makeup items that littered the floor. James bent over to collect a couple of jars that were close to him. The last can had a silver top that had rolled a couple of inches away from the base of the product. He read the label on the front: Pond's Cold Cream. A sort of face makeup. He remembered that Anne had used it when they lived together. Ruth took the mascaras and lipsticks she had picked up and put them inside the metallic cabinet of the powder room. Her brow furrowed as she looked around.

"Missing something?" James asked. He showed her the cream. "I can help clean up for you if you have somewhere you need to be."

Ruth smiled. "That won't be necessary, Mr. Anderson. Thank you, nevertheless." She took the opal-colored jar from James. When James didn't leave, she continued. "You see, I'm supposed to deliver this expensive one to Miss Kingston. Mr. Cross had me pick it up for her in case she ran out." Ruth snorted. "How pretentious is she? No honest woman needs makeup, and certainly a maid like me doesn't have a use for this poison."

James crossed his arms. "Poison?"

"Don't be dim-witted." She tapped the jar with her finger. "You probably have no idea what's even in this."

"And you do?" James teased.

"Perhaps." Ruth winked, walking toward Elizabeth's room. "Now, if you don't mind, I have a lot to do around here."

James walked after her. "Actually, I have a few questions for you regarding Fiona."

"Fiona? I had nothing to do with that." Ruth held the jar closer to her chest.

"You work for the Cross family, do you not?"

"Yes, of course."

"Undoubtedly the family would try to protect one another, so I was wondering if perhaps you have any insight into their dynamic?"

"You could say they are all the assertive type. Almost too determined for their own good, whether it is to make ends meet or look pretty for the press. A flame such as that is bound to burn out eventually." She shifted the jar to one hand and let her other arm drop to her side.

"Do you like working for them?"

Ruth thought for a moment. "The Cross family is an exquisite name brand. It's an honor." Her smile wavered.

"Have you been working for them for long?"

Ruth looked into the distance before turning back at James. "About a year. Time goes by awfully slow when every day has nothing to look forward to."

"You could always leave." James put his hands into his pockets. "Although I have to say, it always catches up with you in some way or another."

"Talking from experience?" Ruth chuckled. "As much as it could be better, it could always be worse. I'm content in this miniature purgatory I live in."

James took in the thin frame of the young woman, her ferocity both amusing and unsettling.

"Do you have a close relationship with Roger?"

She crossed her arms. "I wouldn't label it in that manner. I simply work for the Cross estate."

"I saw you go into Roger's compartment after we bumped into each other in the—"

"Each other? I think you're forgetting what happened. You foolishly backed into me."

"I am very sorry about that." James leaned against the wall. "What were you helping Roger with?"

"This is a very roundabout way to say you've been watching me." She smiled, amused. "I asked for a folder for Alexander. That man is a slob above all else, but I couldn't care less about what they have going on as long as I get my pay."

"What was it he told you to retrieve?"

"What does it matter to you?" Ruth challenged.

"I'm curious."

"Then go and ask him yourself, if you're so keen." She looked around, then whispered. "Between you and me, I think whatever it was, he wanted to make sure it was still there."

James moved closer to hear her whisperings. "What would be so important?"

Ruth shrugged. "I heard Alexander and Fiona arguing about something the other night. Fiona stormed out of the room furious. I wouldn't have wanted to be him. Not like he cares though, he has his painted monkey, Miss Kingston."

"What do you have against Miss Kingston?"

"It's not her I really worry about, it's these men. Looking down on women. Elizabeth is becoming more like them every day. Just like the men, she can get violent when she drinks too much." Ruth rolled up her sleeve to show a purple and yellow bruise. "I'll have to get used to calling her Mrs. Cross soon enough. Who would've imagined that?" Ruth shook her head and then walked past James, who made no effort to stop her.

"Miss Crown—"

"I swear, if you call me by my surname, I am going to give you a bruise to match mine." She cracked a smile, but her eyes retained their intense nature.

James's smile straightened into a thin line as he looked at Ruth's bruise. "Where were you when Fiona was killed? Did she ask for you before she went to bed?"

"No, she never called me, which was probably why I forced myself to stay up as late as I could before passing out. Not really passing out, I just mean collapsing from exhaustion. It's only the three of us staffing this train—me, the conductor, Dean. I was cleaning all day and then I had to check the stockroom to make sure all the arrangements for breakfast had been labeled and ready to cook. There was also a new shipment for the train from The Armstrong Company when we picked up Miss Kingston." Ruth looked down at the tin.

"When did you go back to your room that night?" James asked.

"I hope you don't think I'm capable of this mess. I was back in my room around two-thirty in the morning. Now, is that all?"

"For now. Thank you for your help."

Ruth nodded, then continued toward Elizabeth's room.

The smell of fresh pastry drifting down the hall made James's mouth water. As he got closer to the dining coach, he could smell cinnamon and melted butter for late afternoon tea. Upon entering, he found Elizabeth sitting next to Clara. The table was set with a red linen tablecloth. Thin, decorative doilies decorated each side of the table, where two large tea trays stood filled with cucumber sandwiches, scones, petit fours, and other dainty pastries.

Walking to the beverage caddy by the window, James poured some hot water into a mug to make tea. Sifting through the tea bags, he found his favorite, English Breakfast. As he was adding cream and sugar, Elizabeth called out to him.

"James, darling, please join us."

James walked over and pulled out a chair. Clara stood up to leave.

"Oh, please do stay." Elizabeth held on to Clara's arm playfully.

Clara shook her off and flashed her eyes in James's direction.

"Thank you for tea, Elizabeth," Clara responded indignantly.

Elizabeth smiled sweetly. "Of course. We should do this again tomorrow. With my busy schedule, I normally never have time to sit down and have tea."

Clara placed her napkin next to her plate and left without a response.

Elizabeth sighed. "It has been such a long day, for you too, I suppose. And about earlier, I am so embarrassed for how I behaved. You must forgive me. It must be this train. I haven't been myself. I feel … out of tune."

James nodded, bringing the mug to his lips. "Happens to the best of us."

Elizabeth looked rather pleased with herself as she pushed her hair behind her ear. "What brings you here anyhow? Aboard the train, specifically."

"I'm returning to North Conway."

"That's it? How vague and yet intriguing, fascinating almost." She smiled. "And you're a copper, so I've heard."

James watched her eyes look him up and down. He was preparing to answer when she cut him off.

"Well, you better be on your toes. I can't say any of us are free of a guilty conscience. Only now, someone has gone a little too far." Elizabeth took a sip of tea, then placed her teacup back down on its saucer, a smile passing her lips.

James blew across his tea, bobbing the tea bag as if he were fishing. "In my opinion, guilt is a mind killer. The way it gnaws on your conscience is like how a dog gnaws on its bone. After all, it is the most irreversible act."

"Relax, darling." Elizabeth crossed her legs as she reached for a scone.

"Speaking of this matter, would you be opposed to

answering a few questions about where you were last night?" James asked.

"Of course. It is the next step in these silly investigations. I recently watched *Champion of Lost Causes* at the movie palace in Suffern. You may have heard of the place; it was previously called the Lafayette Theatre. Anyway, from the movie I figured that is how these murder investigations are supposed to be done. Silent films are marvelous, even in the absence of words you can see everything with just a gesture. In this one, Edmund Lowe had to figure out a murder in a gambling club."

James rested his chin on his left hand as he swirled the tea bag in his mug. "Interesting. I haven't had the chance to see it yet."

"You simply must. When we get back to New York, I will have Alexander organize a viewing for you."

"Thank you, but that's not necessary."

Elizabeth eyed him suspiciously. "Isn't this whole crime business right up your alley?"

James straightened his back. "Just because I am part of the police does not mean I enjoy crime."

"If you say so, copper." There was a pause. "Well let's get on with this, I haven't got all day."

"This shouldn't take too long. I want to piece together everyone's account of the night."

"Do you think it's possible to forget something you've done?"

"Depends on what that thing is. I would say that if you don't remember murdering someone, odds are you are on something strong, and even then, I don't think you'd forget taking someone's life."

"You're right, of course. Unless you've murdered so many people you forget." Elizabeth smirked.

"We try to catch those people before they have too many to remember."

"You try." Elizabeth placed emphasis on the two words as she repeated them. "I think it is rather dim for someone to write something on Fiona's arm, though. How cliché. Especially that date."

"What date?" James watched her, letting the silence linger.

Elizabeth looked out the window, pinching her fingertips in her satin gloves. "I guess I shouldn't have said anything. Roger told me when he went into the room he saw numbers on her arm. I was pretty drunk, but that's something I remember he told me."

"When did he tell you that it was a date?"

"Is this important? I thought you would've seen it already. You really call yourself a detective? Well, at any rate, you're not a very good one."

James put his mug down on the table a little too hard, causing her to jump. The hard lines on his forehead softened as he watched her recompose herself and sit up straight. "I'm sorry, the lack of sleep must be showing." James put a hand through his copper hair, its thickness hiding the dried blood still freckled there.

"It was around three in the morning when Roger knocked on Alexander's door. I heard them arguing something dreadful. Alexander's room is right next to mine. It connects. I had him change rooms so he would be closer to me. I didn't trust Fiona. It always felt like she was hiding something from all of us. Why, I wouldn't be surprised if she had an entirely different life. When I went in to speak with the brothers, Roger said something about a date of some kind on her arm."

"So, you went to see them at 3:00 a.m., or after?"

"I don't know. At three maybe. While they hollered, I

laid on his couch. I was too far gone to remember anything else besides mention of some date. I must have drifted to sleep in Alexander's room when they were talking."

"I see. Well, Elizabeth, do you know what the date signifies?"

"All this talk has made me tired. I think you better ask Roger about the date. I don't remember what it was or why this nonsense is relevant."

"Then I will. As for your whereabouts, what were your movements last night?"

"The better question is where wasn't I last night." Elizabeth laughed for a moment. Upon seeing James unamused, she sighed and pouted her lips. "I was getting ready for the party at eight. Alexander picked me up at my compartment around nine, and we walked to the party. That's when I ran into you and turned on some jazz. I was hoping to sing my newest song, 'Lavender Lilies.' Would you like to hear it?"

"Perhaps tonight," James said, watching Elizabeth beam. "Where were you after you left?"

Elizabeth scratched her head thrice. "I believe Alexander and I walked to the back of the train for some fresh air before returning to our compartments to sleep."

"How long have you known Alexander?"

"For a while now. We met at a saloon many years ago. I sang on Thursday nights to get extra money. My parents never approved of a career in singing."

"I heard Alexander was your agent. Do you like working with him, or are you switching managers?"

"Now, what's the point of asking all these questions if you already know the answers?" Elizabeth shook her head.

James grimaced as a tinge of pink rose in his cheeks.

"I do like working with him. Two peas in a pod, we are." She smiled.

"Is that something Mrs. Cross would have agreed with?"

Elizabeth's smile faded as her eyes shifted down to her teacup. James instantly regretted asking. As much as he needed to know the answer, it didn't make asking the question any easier.

"Probably not. Oh, I shouldn't have said that. Not with her having passed and all. My—" She stopped for a moment. "My mother always said to respect the dead." The end of Elizabeth's sentence came out in no more than a whisper.

"Did you know Mrs. Cross well?" James continued.

"She was simply charming, playful."

"I have to say, you make her seem no better than a child."

"I suppose it would come across that way. I didn't know her well. She seemed more ornamental than a partner of his. He admitted to me once he only married her for her money, but perhaps that was the drink talking. You see, I know I won't find true love. Frankly, I don't believe it exists. Not for people like me anyway. Being a celebrity means whoever I marry, I will never truly know if they are marrying me for love or for my money and fame. And in any event, I don't want anyone to be in my way."

"You seem to have a very close relationship with Alexander. Do you think Fiona or Roger thought you and Alexander were in an intimate relationship?"

"Honestly, I don't care what they think. The same goes for the press. They can tarnish me all they want, but that doesn't change who I know I am. And who Alexander knows me as, which is much more important. I love Roger with all my heart, in a platonic way. He was the first person to give me a chance by letting me work at his club. That's where I first met Alexander. Oh, what I'd give to go back to simpler times. No expectations. No rules. It's a lot less forgiving when millions of people are watching your every move. You can't make one wrong step or your name is burned from people's memories, and you have to change your name and start over. Easier said than done, mind you. As much as it might be tempting to start over, there are a few things that bring me back to this lifestyle. A few people, specifically."

Elizabeth winked and took a strand of hair out from behind her ear. "Alexander always knows how to keep me on track. He is the first man to see me as something more than just this." She gestured with her hands over her body. "Men can be such vile creatures sometimes. I must be fair, though, so can women. Humanity itself."

"Even so, there is good in the world. And I like to think that people are not so easily classified as "good" or "evil." We all have our dark moments."

"I suppose I should take heart in your words. Coppers see the worst in people, yet here you are. How do you get through it?"

"Every day is a new day. I try remembering there is still good in people, and it's worth fighting for family, friends, and loved ones."

"What happens if you lose all of that?"

"You keep going. I see everyone as someone to fight for. People are extremely social beings, and it's almost selfish to not see how everyone is related to another. Everyone is someone's daughter, son, mother, father, partner, or friend. I fight for them with that in mind. Fiona was Alexander's wife and—"

Elizabeth shuddered and wrapped her arms around herself. James paused and watched as she took a sip of her tea, letting the warmth rejuvenate her body.

"Do you love Alexander?" James asked. "I know it's a hard question."

Elizabeth tilted her head and sighed. "Alexander and Roger are the only ones who could truly love me, because they knew me before all of this. Not that they do," Elizabeth responded, her voice growing soft. "The only permanent relationship I'm in is with my career. Alexander has respect for my talents. He knows a rare gift when he sees it. We are partners who both want the same things and will do whatever it takes to get there. I won't risk a relationship with him when it could break me."

James was quiet for a moment. It was clear that he would have to speak with Alexander again. "It was brought to my attention you had some interest in a letter opener. Silver and ornamented with rubies from—"

"The Kingdom of Fife in Scotland. No, I didn't steal it." Elizabeth rolled her eyes. "I can tell you've been talking to Clara. I must have heard about that ridiculous letter opener a thousand times. To her, that letter opener is the crown jewels. She thinks I stole it. It's outrageous. I could buy hundreds of rubies if I wanted. It makes me laugh. She's lost that thing more times than I can count. If she's blaming me again, she must have lost it."

"Why would she blame you?"

Elizabeth threw her hands up. "It seems like I'm always the one to be blamed since I'm not part of the family. Not like she is by blood; she also worked to be a part of it. You'd think after everything I've done for this family, I would be more appreciated."

"What have you done for the family?"

"I've saved them from debt and poverty time and again. Those Cross brothers don't appreciate anything."

"Were you, by any chance, ever jealous of Mrs. Cross because she was part of the family and you are not?"

"Me? Jealous? I am not jealous of her. She had her mysteries and meaningless ways of life, and what has her life amounted to? I have always been better than her. A career, wealth that is my own, beauty, fame. I have everything. If anything, I feel sorry for her. Now, if that is all, I promised I would meet with Roger." Elizabeth got up and began to walk out of the room.

"Wait, Elizabeth." He got up quickly to follow her, but in doing so spilled tea onto his lap. He placed his mug on the table and looked for a napkin. Seeing Clara's crumpled napkin on the table, he picked it up to blot the tea. While unfolding the napkin, a piece of paper fluttered to the ground.

Picking it up, James turned the paper over to find a note.

*Clara,*
*Tonight at 7*

He pocketed the message, thinking the lettering looked eerily like the note that was left under his door. He walked back to his compartment, figuring he might as well check to be sure. Taking out his key, he unlocked the door and closed it behind him. He picked up Anne's copy of *Alice's Adventures in Wonderland* and opened it to the front page. Upon comparison, he confirmed the note he received earlier matched the one written to Clara. James went to close the book but noticed there appeared to be a new note poking out of the pages. A raw anger grew in his throat. He looked to the window to clear his mind before pulling the note from the book. This note was not handwritten like the other ones, but rather was ripped out of a book.

> She heard it from her cave. She is Hecate, with the
> splendid headband. And the Lord Helios heard
> it too, the magnificent son of Hyperion.

# Chapter Seven

James felt the typeface of the print before creasing the paper and pocketing it. He exited his compartment and walked toward the dining coach, which had been set up for the evening meal. It was hard to believe the room was a place for eating rather than a photoshoot, with all the expensive silver placed meticulously against the dark oak table and red tablecloth. The chandelier remained steady despite the rigorous speed the train was going to trek through the mountain pass. He stepped closer to the window, lined in gold and green curtains, to peer out at the pine trees drowning in the ombre shades of violet, red, and orange from the fading sun. James jumped as a hand landed on his right shoulder and turned to see Alexander.

"Nights like these are rare and few. This is when I feel reinvigorated. Like I could do anything. Be anyone."

"And what is it you would like to do?" James asked politely, adjusting the cuffs of his shirtsleeves.

"Anything. Just start over entirely."

"I didn't expect to find you two here." Elizabeth's silky

red dress moved fluidly as she strode into the room like a gazelle. The light reflecting off her blue eyes, she looked James up and down. "Are you going to fix that mop on your head?"

James put a hand up instinctively to his hair.

She winked before lightly hitting his arm. "Oh, I'm just teasing. You always look fine."

"What is it you want, Elizabeth?" Alexander asked. He clasped the back of a chair and maintained his rigid composure as she moved toward him. Her thin dress accentuated her hips as she swayed side to side, like a serpent preparing to strike.

"I don't think going outside is that big of a commitment." She smiled, laying her hand on top of his. He shook her off.

"You'll have to go alone. I can't risk getting sick on your account."

Elizabeth withdrew her arm. "On my account? What would you have without me?" she snapped.

"Peace of mind, with a dash of sanity." Alexander smiled before walking toward the bar. "James, do you want anything to drink?" he asked over his shoulder, picking up a glass.

Before James could respond, Elizabeth walked next to Alexander and hit the crystal he was holding out of his hand.

"What was that for?" Alexander cried.

"You know damn well. Damn well."

"Not in front of our guest, dear. Maybe you should take a rest, you do look awfully pale. You must be worn out." Alexander pushed back a strand of her hair, seemingly unconcerned about the glass shattered around him.

Elizabeth's face soured, hands clenched at her sides.

Alexander laughed and looked at James. "Women. They're a different breed. You never know what's going on inside their heads."

Elizabeth turned her snarl into a smile. "Men like you are the bane of women everywhere." Her eyes flashed as she turned to James. "Come on." She looped her arm through James's and led him out.

Once they made it to the caboose, Elizabeth let go of him. "I'm sorry you had to hear all of that."

"That's alright." James opened the door to the outside area and had Elizabeth walk in front of him. As the wind from the winter night made it hard to hear one another, they remained side by side.

"It's a lucky chance we're alone like this now. I don't know if I'll have another opportunity to talk to you like this, what with tomorrow being the last night on board. I don't believe Alexander will ever let me ride like this again, with the murder."

"I'm sure he will eventually. He probably just wants to make sure you're safe."

"I've been alright." Elizabeth got close to James's ear to make sure he could hear her. "Alexander has not always been irrevocably suffocating." Elizabeth let out a quick laugh before looking down at her feet. "I don't know what changed, but I don't recognize him anymore." She turned to James. "You wouldn't happen to have a cigarette on you, would you?"

"Sorry, I quit a few years ago," James said, watching her expression.

"You're so disappointing," she jested.

"You're not the first and most definitely won't be the last to say so." James smirked, shifting his body to look at the end of the sunset. "It's beautiful out here. Otherworldly almost."

"My God, please don't start with that." Elizabeth motioned for James to follow her to the black railing at the edge of the train. She pinched the hems of her black gloves before wrapping her hands around the cool iron.

"What do you mean?"

"Alexander goes on and on about how God has painted this heavenly canvas on Earth and how we must deal with our sins and Earthly damnations."

"Earthly damnations?"

"He explains them as something like, 'God has predestined us for the lives we live and what we go through.'"

"Like fate? Is that what you mean?"

"More like, what does Alexander mean? I much prefer the Greek and Roman stuff Roger studied." Elizabeth laughed, then realized James was waiting for her to continue. "Alexander explains it like this: if your father passes away, then God knew you were strong enough to get through it. If you go blind tomorrow, that is the path He chose for you."

James nodded, furrowing his brow as he thought about it.

"I hate it though, that idea, the notion that a God chose me to deal with what I have."

"What about it is so unnerving for you?"

"It's wrong. I made my opportunities. I worked to be where I am today, with no help from a God."

"And you're allowed to think that. Who am I to judge? Religion means the world to a lot of people, and in my own opinion, I think we'd feel a lot more alone without it."

"Do you think everyone can be forgiven?" Elizabeth asked.

"I think forgiveness is always possible. It's not always easy to reach that point, but it's what we should all aim for.

Sometimes it just takes time." James wrapped his hands around the railing, turning to look at Elizabeth, who was lost in her thoughts.

She shook herself awake. "I found something yesterday that made me think about forgiveness."

James watched, perplexed, as Elizabeth reached inside one of her gloves and pulled out a piece of paper.

"Here."

James eagerly took the paper and read.

## Bientôt tout le monde sera au courant de l'éclipse Solaire

"Soon everyone will know about the solar eclipse," he mumbled.

Elizabeth glanced at the note in his hand before looking up to see his expression. "Doesn't make much sense. We all saw the solar eclipse the other day."

James used his index finger to trace over the messy script handwriting. "Where did you find this?"

Elizabeth fixed a lock of hair that had gone astray. "It was in my makeup tin." Her cheeks grew rosy from the biting winds of the night.

"What kind of tin?"

"Pond's Cold Cream. Usually, I pick up my makeup myself—it's something I like to do—but I ran out of time. Alexander had one of the staff members pick it up instead."

James looked up at the starry sky, admiring the cold, white light reflecting from the stars. "Thank you for handing it over. I'll see what I can make of it."

"Of course. As much as I enjoy theatrics, this is one show in which I don't want to play a role."

# Chapter Eight

Martin laughed as James and Elizabeth walked in. "Thought we lost you out in the cold."

"What a pity," Clara added, saluting the pair with her cocktail.

Elizabeth parted from James to walk to her assigned seat next to Alexander. James found his seat at the table next to Martin, whose leg was bouncing erratically. Elizabeth pulled out the vacant chair next to Alexander, but after a moment of hesitation, she pushed it back in and left. If Alexander noticed, he didn't acknowledge it. The rest of the guests' attention was consumed by the sweet scent of a freshly made cinnamon apple pie.

"You missed dinner; it was truly the best venison I've ever had." Martin wiped the crumbs from the corners of his mouth with the back of his hand.

"Hardly," said Alexander, reaching for his napkin.

James looked around the table. "That's quite alright. I seemed to have lost my appetite."

"I'm sure Dean could find you some scraps if you need

something more filling than the pie." Clara finished her cocktail and looked around. "Where is that man?"

"Don't make a fuss over me, I'm fine." James smiled half-heartedly.

Alexander nodded before standing from his seat and excusing himself back to his room. The rest of the guests slowly followed his lead until the room was clear.

James watched Martin with interest. "What's bothering you?"

Martin shrugged. "What did you find? You have this odd sort of look on your face."

"Thanks." James reached across the table to pull the pie closer to him. He used the large knife beside the plate to cut himself a piece.

"I'm serious, what's going on?" Martin folded his hands and rested them on the table.

James reached into his blazer for the thin paper, then handed it to Martin. "Elizabeth gave me this."

Confusion crossed Martin's visage, his eyes scanning across the writing.

"You read French?" James asked.

Martin focused on the note. "Yeah, learned it at school. Columbia University." He paused. "Come with me, I need to check something." Martin jumped up, his chair swinging back and falling to the floor.

"What's the rush?" James asked, watching as Martin hurried into the hallway. James finished his pie quickly before hurrying after Martin.

Martin unlocked the door to his room and beckoned James inside. In turn, James closed the door behind them as Martin lit the light and placed the note on the desk.

"I was afraid of this." Martin pulled open the bottom drawer and placed a new note next to the one from

Elizabeth. James looked at the note Martin had received. It was in text, much like the one placed in James's book.

But when the loud-thunderer, heard this, he sent to Ha<u>d</u>es, the one with the golden wand, the Argos-killer so that he may persuade Had<u>es</u>, with gentle words, that he allow holy Persephone to leave the misty realms of d<u>a</u>rkness and be brought up to the light in order to join the Gods in Olympus, so that her mother may see her with her own eyes and then let go of her anger. Hermes did not disobey, but straightaway he headed down beneath the depths of the Earth, rushing full speed, leaving behind the abode of Olympus. And he found the Lor<u>d</u> inside his palace.

"When did you get this?" James asked, picking up the printed note.

"I found it in my luggage before dinner." Martin took the note back from James. "What do you think this is all about?"

"I don't know. I got another one this afternoon."

Martin groaned. "My God, I can't keep them all straight."

"Maybe that's the point." James put both messages he received on Martin's desk as well. His eyes drifted across the documents.

"What are you brewing up there in that head of yours?" Martin asked.

James looked at the four notes and rearranged them to fit the order they had been received.

Martin picked up the document Elizabeth gave James. "We don't know when Elizabeth found this note; she could have gotten it before one of ours."

James contemplated. "It's hard to say. But I found mine after lunch and you found yours before dinner, so it figures hers would have to be around that time too. She must have found it later in the day, or else she would have given the note to us earlier."

Martin looked back at the notes. "Isn't it rather odd Elizabeth happened to get one? Ours were both unequivocally for us."

"It had to be for her. The makeup was ordered specifically for her."

"Then whoever this is must have known she would show us."

"Unless she wanted us to find it now."

Martin leaned against the wall next to the desk. "You can't be serious."

"Kill Fiona and she would have Alexander all to herself. Although, something about them seemed off tonight. Alexander refused to go outside with her, and she didn't sit with him for dinner." James looked at the documents, placing the one Martin had at the bottom.

**Maintenant, je ferai toujours partie de sa vie.**

She heard it from her cave. She is Hecate, with the splendid headband. And the Lord Helios heard it too, the magnificent son of Hyperion.

**Bientôt tout le monde sera au courant de l'éclipse Solaire.**

. . .

But when the loud-thunderer, heard this, he sent to Hades, the one with the golden wand, the Argos-killer so that he may persuade Hades, with gentle words, that he allow holy Persephone to leave the misty realms of darkness and be brought up to the light in order to join the Gods in Olympus, so that her mother may see her with her own eyes and then let go of her anger. Hermes did not disobey, but straightaway he headed down beneath the depths of the Earth, rushing full speed, leaving behind the abode of Olympus. And he found the Lord inside his palace.

"It's some sort of acronym," James whispered. He asked for Martin's notepad and pen and flipped to a new page before writing down each letter that was underlined.

## SELENE IS DEAD

Martin squinted as he looked over James's shoulder. "I knew this was connected. I knew it." Martin reached for one of his suitcases and quickly unclasped the lock. "I'm sure you've been wondering why we boarded this train. Why I came with you."

"I didn't really think anything of it other than you were writing an article on Elizabeth."

"James, I must say, you're quite gullible. We didn't board this train for you, we boarded it for me. When I overheard Michaels say he was trying to get you to New Hampshire, I proposed he pull in a few favors. I said it would be a great opportunity to keep our eyes on this family after what happened."

James put down the notepad. "What are you talking about?"

"I told you I wanted to write the next big story. Well, there have been whisperings that the Cross family was involved with the case of a missing girl," said Martin.

"When was this case, I've never heard of it."

"No, you wouldn't have. It was more gossip than an actual case. This was a while back. Before Fiona married Alexander. Someone who was arrested in one of the gin joints said Roger kidnapped a girl from another estate; her name was Selene."

James's eyes went wide. "You're only telling me this now?" The words slid through clenched teeth. "Why hold back such an important piece of information?"

"Because it might just be hearsay." Martin raised his hands. "But we can't ignore it now, not with these notes. We need to ask Roger to be sure."

James tried to regain his composure. "Who was this person who reported it? They should have reported it before being arrested, then it might have been taken more seriously."

"The man said his wife was one of the lady's maids on the estate. Knew the ins and outs of the place."

"I imagine the police went around to look."

"Found nothing: no girl, no signs of a struggle, and no one had reported her missing in the first place."

James crossed his arms. "The man probably just wanted to get out of trouble."

"That's what I thought too, until I found that his wife was fired from their service without recommendation a week later. She is still unemployed."

"What are the names of this man and his wife? We can find them when we get off the train." James picked up the pen to write on the notepad, looking up at Martin.

Martin smiled. "That's where it gets interesting. Their names are Frederick and Clara O'Donnell."

~

James and Martin hurried their pace as they walked through the train, the edges of oak gleaming against the moon. Martin balled his fist and knocked on the door to Clara's compartment.

"One moment," a shrill voice called. Soon the door swung open, and Ruth stood with a broom. "I'm sorry, but Mrs. O'Donnell isn't here at the moment." Ruth looked down at her broom and swept onto their shoes, as if beckoning them to leave with the dust.

"That's alright, we will come back later." James gave Martin a look before turning around.

"I've not come this close to be told no by a girl." Martin pushed past Ruth and delved into the drawers in Clara's desk.

"What the Hell are you doing!" James said through gritted teeth as he watched Martin go into the room, turning to Ruth.

"You must be off, sir." Ruth emphasized each syllable carefully, like she had rehearsed saying it.

Martin ignored her as he rifled through more of Clara's files.

"Come on Martin, this is illegal!" James said.

Martin looked up at James, "Ha. You think that matters to me?"

"Sir, I insist you leave at once." Ruth rubbed her left thumb into her palm as she stood next to James by the doorway, unsure what to say next.

Martin's body stiffened as he arched his neck. "I heard

you. And look, I'm still here and not leaving. Now get outta here, this isn't your business."

Ruth stood defiantly in the doorway, her eyes blazing as she looked him up and down. "Everything on this train is my business."

Martin pulled out a letter with a stamp but no address. He held it up to James's face before reading the fine script.

*Selene, my Moon,*
*I will send you what I can and soon I will be able to join*
*you, my dear. Soon we will be together, I promise.*
*Yours Forever,*
*Cross*

"Put. That. Down!"

The high-pitched voice caused both men to look up. Clara stood in the doorway. She had changed into a forest green dress with white fringe at the bottom, which cut off under her knee. She turned to Ruth with an accusing glare.

"I told them to leave, honest. I did all I could," Ruth cried.

"I suppose nothing can keep these two out. Dear, why don't you run along now."

Clara moved forward, a bewitching smile holding the men still as Ruth scurried into the hallway. Clara's aged hands knitted themselves together, the fringe of her dress tauntingly following her small steps toward Martin. She turned her gaze from the men to the thin sheet of paper in Martin's sweaty hands.

"I was going to hand that in later at a more opportune

time," Clara said, snatching the paper. "Away from the prying eyes of the press."

Martin snorted. "Who would care about you? You're nothing but a washed-up dame."

Her smile faltered. "If you didn't care, you wouldn't be at my desk looking through my things. It's that simple. You better prepare yourself, Martin. Next thing you know, you might be out of a job." She smirked and turned to James. "Only joking, of course. That's what all of this is. Fun and games."

"I'm sorry we intruded. We can find you later." James nudged Martin and started toward the door.

Clara put her hand on James's arm. "I don't mind your company. Just not that foul dog you have licking at your heels. Now get out, dog. I would like to have a few words with James."

"What would your husband say?" Martin mocked.

Clara struck Martin with the back of her hand. "I think you need to be hit with something harder, but for now this will do."

Martin took it jovially. "I think I did more damage to you than you did to me."

Clara huffed. "Maybe you should lose a few pounds then."

"I'll meet with you later, James."

James nodded, watching as Martin slid back into the corridor.

Clara turned to James. "I haven't a clue who this note was intended for, but I figured you would do well with it. Perhaps it could help."

"Where did you come across it?"

"I found it thrown away in the dining compartment. I couldn't help my curiosity." She clicked her tongue. "I have to believe it's connected to the murder, as well the thievery of my beloved letter opener," she added in emphasis. "Have you any updates?"

"Unfortunately, no, but I will keep my eyes peeled. Until then, it seems you may be familiar with a name we both came across."

Clara let go of James's arm, walked to a red chair and took a seat. "What's the name?" Clara tucked a curl behind her ear

"Selene. Do you know anyone who goes by that name?"

She folded her arms.

"You know the Cross family well, so I was wondering if you knew if there was anyone in their employ named Selene? A relative? Maybe a family friend?" James continued.

"There must be hundreds of people named Selene."

"If the name is as popular as you say, you must come across it often," James said.

"Yes. But I don't know of any that would be this relevant."

"So, it would come as a surprise if your name was linked to hers in some capacity?" James watched as Clara shot up from her seat, starting to walk to the door. "Everything I'm doing is to aid the investigation. I don't want to intrude in your affairs, but I must know what is going on here. For Fiona."

She reached for the doorknob but hesitated, her gaze focused on the knob. "Fiona wouldn't want any of us to be in this position. She had more than enough whispering and secrets herself. As we all do. You should be ashamed of yourselves for intruding on these familial matters. Family is everything," Clara said, turning around to look at James.

"You're the one who has intruded on familial matters," James replied.

Clara tilted her head, her eyes staring daggers. "What did you just say to me?"

"You said before that you worked under Fiona, and the entire Cross estate."

"Yes. That is why my hands look the way they do." Clara exposed her right hand, her rough skin a patchwork of calluses and scars.

"Why are you not coming clean about the Selene matter?" James pressed, pushing down any thoughts his hunch was wrong.

"I'm unsure what you're asking."

"Please, Mrs. O'Donnell, answer the question. There was a report about a girl being kidnapped by Roger; she went by the name Selene."

"That's preposterous."

"Not according to your husband, who reported it after being arrested at a speakeasy."

Clara sighed. "Damn him. Damn him! That fool. He never listened to what I said. Had it all backward." She walked back to the chair and leaned into it.

"Who was Selene?" James asked again.

"I'm getting to it." She paused, looking out the window. "Yes, I knew Selene. The sickly child. I thought after all this time that name was forgotten, like that child was when she was adopted. Not kidnapped," Clara clarified. She raised her brows and her owllike eyes bore into James.

"Did Roger adopt her, what was his involvement? Who would sign off as Cross? It could be either of the brothers."

Clara put her hands out in front of her. "No. Stop with the questions, listen for the answers." She waited for a moment. "Selene lived with my friend and his wife for a time. We thought it would be the best way to keep her birth parents a secret."

"Who were her birth parents?"

Clara sent him a glare before continuing. "Selene's true parents were Roger and Fiona. She was born in 1900."

James wrapped his right hand over his mouth to hide his expression.

"But like I said, Selene was a sickly child, and when pneumonia came around in her third winter, she didn't make it. My friends were aching from the lost, and I told them I could be the only one to know of her death. I couldn't risk anyone finding out. It would break Roger's heart to know his girl had died."

"The note refers to Selene as if she is alive and well. Why would anyone write to her now if she is supposedly dead?"

"Ask the parents. Although now only one lives, not two. You will never know Fiona's story."

James felt a chill travel down his spine. "When Selene was alive, she was sickly?"

"It is a pity, but yes. I had to ask the Cross family for cash to pay for the doctors, medicine, anything she needed. Even after she died, that wretched child put me under. Carrying the burden of such an enormous secret required a trade-off, especially when they let me go for my husband's mistake during his arrest. I needed the money to support myself. The Cross family goes back for generations and wealth is not something they lack. It was only fair. A little off the top won't hurt him."

"Won't hurt Roger, you mean," James clarified. "But it's been twenty-five years since she was born. Does he think you are still supporting her? This entire operation could become a blackmail scheme for the leverage you hold over him." James's shoulders tightened. "It did, didn't it, Moon Swallow."

Clara's face paled. "I think I'm doing what's right by not telling him the truth. He never wanted to get rid of his girl in the first place, but Fiona—" Clara stood and straightened her dress before beckoning him to stand.

James obliged, but said, "I have a few more questions."

"But I have nothing left to say." Clara's voice shook. As her eyes clouded, she walked him to the door. She leaned against the compartment door as a tear streaked down her face and dangled off her chin. She grunted to clear the phlegm in her throat. "I'm sure you will be back soon, in any event." Clara opened the door for him, averting her eyes to the floor.

James nodded, taking a few steps forward before the compartment door slammed at his back. He stood still for a moment, grabbing onto the wall as the train wheels rolled over something on the track. He turned to walk back to his room and found Martin waiting outside a couple paces past the door. "Are you two done, I was beginning to think you'd never be able to escape her."

"What are you doing?" James whispered, his voice dry.

"Trying to hear what you two lovebirds were talking about."

"Oh, close your head." James smiled. "You're lucky she didn't come out with me."

Martin grinned. "What would she do, hit me with her handbag? Throw her jewelry at me? That ruby collar never comes off her."

"That's true." James scratched his ear as he walked down the corridor. "Clara began wearing Fiona's ruby necklace the day after her death. The letter opener also had rubies in it. What associates Fiona with red rubies? It is too much of a coincidence."

Martin shrugged. "Everyone has a color they like, that looks good on them. That is their color."

"Clara said she has been wearing rubies because the color red is strong, like Fiona. What if this isn't about color? Clara said when I spoke to her after Fiona's death that emeralds were her stone, but there are lots of gems that are green besides emeralds." James opened the door to his compartment for Martin.

"What does it matter? Women like jewels. This is starting to sound like what Clara was selling to us about Victorian jewelry."

"That's precisely it, Martin." James hit his arm lightly as he walked through the door to sit on the couch. "It's a type of symbol. Emeralds and rubies, they're both birthstones. Clara's birthday is in May, therefore, her birthstone would be an emerald."

"What about Fiona?" Martin said, taking his notepad out of his pocket along with his pencil. "Her birthday was last month, and December's birthstone is blue topaz."

James closed the door behind him before sitting on the couch beside Martin. "Rubies are the birthstone for July."

"Who is born in July?" Martin asked.

James furrowed his brow. "Clara told me Selene was born in 1900, then died from pneumonia when she was three. We know Fiona's murder was a crime of passion, and it all revolves around this child who passed away. Those numbers carved into Fiona's arm must be the child's birthday. Instead of 71200, it could be July 12th, 1900. Whoever did it knows about Selene and the connection with Fiona. The murderer wrote the date to make a point. I think Roger is the one we need to get answers from. Selene is his illegitimate daughter, after all."

"Was," Martin corrected.

"I'm not so sure she is dead."

"Are you serious?" Martin raised a brow, more in excitement than curiosity.

"We can't take everything Clara said at face value. That letter didn't seem like it was for someone who was dead. I suppose we will have to see what Roger knows."

"We will have to assess for ourselves what everyone knows about Selene. We can scratch off that Clara knew about the child," Martin said.

"Since Clara knew, we could suspect the entire family did as well. Which means everyone could have known about Roger and Fiona's affair. Could she be telling the truth about them?"

Martin gave him a look. "I don't think she is lying about that. You must trust me on this one. Sifting through gossip and rumors for the press has given me a lot of insight. I mean, did you look at Roger's face when he saw her laying there dead. Without a doubt their relationship was something more."

"We need more than that to be sure. To have an affair revealed would have created a lot of tension in the household. Families like the Cross family would have done everything to hold on to their image and reputation," said James.

Martin made a quick entry in his notepad. "I think the bigger question is to ask why Fiona would be murdered now. If we follow the stereotypical route and accuse her husband, like Alexander presumed, it doesn't make sense for him to wait all this time to murder his wife. But who else would gain from her death?"

"When I spoke to Elizabeth, she said Roger and Alexander were the only ones who could truly love her, since they knew her before she became rich and famous," James said.

Martin sneered. "Why on Earth would she have the hots for those two?"

James sighed. "Do you think it's possible Alexander is having an affair with her? She did ask Alexander to put her compartment next to his. By separating them, it would be easier to kill Fiona."

"Perhaps he wanted to bump off his wife himself, that could be why he separated her. That way he would avoid suspicion by not sharing a room with her," Martin said thoughtfully.

"Alexander is a Christian; he would have committed adultery by being involved with Elizabeth."

"Really? I never would have pegged him as such. Adultery. Isn't that a sin?"

"One of the ten commandments, yes. Even so, being an adulterer doesn't mean one is a murderer," James pointed out. "Besides, we don't have any evidence of them having an affair. We should ask him about Selene and if he knew about her. Perhaps this way we can verify Clara's tale before we talk with Roger."

"We need to ask him if he is having an affair with Elizabeth too," Martin said, finding new authority in his voice.

# Chapter Nine

James shook his head. "That will be a pleasant conversation. 'Hello, Alex. We heard you've been cheating on your wife. What do you have to say about that?'"

Martin rolled his eyes. "We won't word it like that."

"I'm just saying, no matter how you word it, it's not good." James stood and walked toward the door to leave.

"If we can prove this accusation, then that would be a nail in the coffin," Martin stressed.

"We have no reason to believe they're having an affair. Nothing concrete. Again, we can't completely trust what Clara said about Selene." James motioned for Martin to walk with him down the hall.

Martin followed. "What's her gain to lie to us?"

"I don't know. She could be trying to throw us off her by blaming someone else."

"You think Clara is trying to use this murder to get back at the family?"

James shrugged. As they reached Alexander's door, he

whispered, "For now, we're focusing on the name Selene. That's it." James rapped his knuckles against the door.

"It's unlocked," Alexander said from the inside.

Martin took out his notepad and pencil from his jacket pocket, grinning. "We'll see what comes up."

James reached for the doorknob and pushed the door open. The atmosphere was somber, as heavy hues of crimson and gold wallpaper dressed the room, a soft luminescence growing from two small lamps. Alexander looked at the men expectedly, holding a bottle of white wine in his hand.

"What can I do for you gentlemen?" He shifted his weight onto his right leg, and a smile crawled across his face.

"We would like to ask you some questions," James said as he walked into the space.

"More questions? God help me. Well, get on with it. Ask away," Alexander mocked, looking between James and Martin before returning his attention to the wine.

While he poured, he raised the bottle to increase the length of the stream until the golden alcohol reached the meniscus of his glass. Once the glass was filled, he whipped his head back to Martin, who was standing in the doorway beside a crucifix. "Martin, please decide whether you are joining in this conversation or not. If you'd like to stay, close the door."

Martin pinched his lips together as he took a step forward, his shadow lingering on the wall as he turned to close the door behind him. Once it was done, he concentrated on his notes and flicked through a few pages of his notepad before leaning against the door.

"Ah, there we go." Alexander brought the glass carefully to his lips and took a sip. "Now ask your questions and be gone. I do not like my time being wasted."

James looked around the small room and settled himself into a plush maroon chair with clawed feet. "This is a hard topic to breach."

"You're asking for money, aren't you?" Lines ebbed across Alexander's forehead.

"No," James said, the word sounding more like a question than a statement.

Alexander sighed as he rolled his eyes to Martin. "A publicity stunt, then?"

Martin cracked a joint in his finger, causing James to wince from the dreadful sound. "Let's get on with it, shall we." Martin licked the tip of his pencil. "We heard about your relationship with —"

"We're focusing on Selene, remember?" James firmly stated, giving Martin a warning glare.

Martin scoffed in rebuttal as he faced Alexander. "We know about your affair, and we would like to talk to you about it. How it may be related to Fiona's murder."

Martin and James watched Alexander place his wine glass on the oak table before him with a sure grip, a vein throbbing between his fingers. James pinched the bridge of his nose and looked to the ceiling, wishing he was somewhere else.

Alexander looked incredulous as he stood and faced Martin. "You're accusing me of having an affair? That's always how these things turn up, you snoopers accusing the gracious husbands of infidelity. Like Adam and Eve, man must take the fall for women's inadequacies and lust. And you, why you're one to talk, as you killed your wife two years ago." A grin crept along the edges of Alexander's lips as the tips of Martin's ears turned red.

Martin erupted in a torrent of anger as he threw his notepad and pencil to the ground and moved toward

Alexander, who was relishing in his victory. James rushed to put himself between the two men.

"Fighting is not going to do any of us good. We're here to figure out what happened to Fiona."

"How dare you make accusations against me," Martin spat, disregarding James as if he was no more than a figment of his imagination. "I wouldn't have laid a finger on my wife. That's more than you can say."

Alexander snickered. "Go run along now before you get hurt, you hypocrite."

"You're not worth my time." Martin huffed as he straightened his shirt, trying to master his emotions.

"I think we need to start this discussion over, Alexander," James said.

"You better."

"We found evidence that someone signing off as 'Cross' was writing to a woman—"

Alexander turned to look out the windows, folding his hands behind his back. "It's my brother, Roger, no doubt. He always seemed to make the wrong choices. We all knew it was coming. He could never stop going after my … leftovers." He turned to pick up the crystal glass again, letting the cool stem drape across his knuckle.

"Leftovers?" Martin interjected.

Alexander brushed away the thought as if it were a cobweb. "I knew about the little thing he and Fiona had. I believe the Lord works in mysterious ways. We must follow the path He has chosen for each of us. I can only hope He will grant His forgiveness to us all, which extends to my wife and brother." He straightened his glass and drank.

"You don't seem very upset. Your wife broke one of your ten commandments," Martin remarked, remembering the point James made earlier.

"Very good. I didn't know you were so up on your

scripture." Alexander took another sip of wine and swirled the drink in the form of a figure eight, his eyes transfixed on its movement. "I was told it was one night, not that it is an excuse. But again, only God can judge."

"One night?" James paused. "We were told—"

Alexander put his hand up to silence him. "Don't take me for a fool. I know that's a lie. You see, Roger owns this club, Hexate, where drinks flow just as quickly as the money that flows out of that place. Gambling, women, it's a place of sin I've been begging him to shut down for years." Alexander's eyes glazed over, lost in thought. "I finally saw them together, my wife and my brother, after the bartender told me he caught them in Roger's office. I swear I briefly lost my mind, becoming nearly as mad as Hamlet. But then I saw her."

"Her? Fiona?" James raised a brow.

Alexander's smile widened. "She saved me from doing something I truly would've regretted. She sang like an angel. The dark violet curtains on either side of the stage illuminated her diamond figure in the lights like a vampire. Perhaps she is more of an incubus than a Godly figure. It was like she was calling out to me. Her voice paralyzed me. I couldn't resist her." He paused for a moment to finish his drink. "She was like a heap of clay, simply waiting for someone to mold her and share her talents with the world."

"So, you had an affair with this woman?" Martin pestered, watching as James sat down.

"Affair? Never. Are you even listening? I'm a man of God. The way her hair gleaned in the light, her blue dress swaying rhythmically while hugging her waist. She was a supernatural figure I dare not touch." He paused for a moment to put his glass down, folding his hands together. "We talked all night. I couldn't get enough of her voice. It rang bright like little silver bells when she laughed. We came from two different worlds, but I connected to her more than I had ever connected to anyone. She is a once in a lifetime kind of woman, and I'm just the fortunate lonely soul who ran into her on a cold November night."

"Was it Selene?" James asked, hoping that was where the conversation was heading.

Alexander walked over to the chair opposite the one James sat in. "Ah, if she was Selene, then I would have begged to be her Endymion." He smiled. The tips of his grin fell as he shook himself awake from the fantasy. "I thought it would be obvious—that woman was Elizabeth."

"What was she like when you first met her?"

"Life changing." Alexander said.

"For her too, I reckon," Martin added, bending over to pick up the notepad and pencil he'd thrown.

"Have you ever heard of a woman named Selene? In connection with Elizabeth, Fiona, or any the family?" James asked.

Alexander crossed his legs. "Roger has a lot of women working for him at his place, both servers and performers. He would be the best person for you to talk to about these matters."

"Roger never married?" Martin asked.

"No, always said he was waiting for the right girl. The fool still believes there is such a thing as love." Alexander grimaced.

"And you don't?" James said.

"Love is for children and fairy tales. The only way to get ahead in the world is to find a strong business partner for a wife. Women have a particular charm over the male sex that can be most useful." He stood to pour another glass of wine.

"It goes both ways," Martin countered.

Alexander shrugged over the white wine he was pouring. "You know what I mean."

Martin analyzed Alexander's shifting expression before responding sincerely. "I feel sorry for you. What kind of human existence are you living that does not include love?"

"Between me and Roger, he has always been the fantasist. Sometimes it works out for him, other times not so much." Alexander turned with his glass and watched as James picked at a hangnail beside his cuticle.

"What makes you say that?" James said, stopping the motion.

"Roger got written out of mother's estate for not following the rules. He has always been a familial embarrassment." Alexander squinted to emphasize his point.

"What could he have done to deserve that?" Martin asked.

"Roger was stealing jewelry and taking out loans faster than anyone could imagine. He needed money and sold what he could from the estate. No one in the family knew where that money was going. It was easier to not think about it." Alexander lifted his glass, the curvature of the wine bending to his lips as he drank.

"Did Roger know he was written out of the will?" James asked.

"No, not for a long time. But when our dear old mother passed, well, I couldn't keep it from him forever."

"So, what did he say when you confronted him about it?" Martin pressed.

"Nothing. Simply stood up and walked off, for a smoke I thought. When I came home that evening, our grandfather's memoriam from the Spanish-American War was missing. Everything of value was lost. It nearly killed our grandmother when we figured out that Roger was the thief. God bless her soul. While I haven't asked him directly about its whereabouts, I have reason to believe it's all long gone. Sold to some underground networks, perhaps."

"Would you be able to recognize it, given the chance?" James asked.

Alexander laughed. "I'd like to think so. Though I doubt that will happen any time soon. Roger is not a prideful man, as he began to borrow money from Elizabeth. I'm sure you know about that. It will be all in the press, isn't that right, Martin?" Alexander winked, taking a sip of his drink.

Martin smirked. "Of course."

Alexander placed the glass down. "Good sport. It may not be good news but being on the front page is worth the gossip. You might be able to make us your next headline."

"That all depends on how the rest of this unfolds," Martin said, tearing his eyes from his writing.

"Well, let us think. Selene, you say. Fiona had a cousin named Selene, before she passed."

"And when did this Selene pass?" Martin asked.

"You know, I can't be sure. Family wasn't a topic Fiona liked to discuss." Alexander cracked his knuckle.

"Were your families close before you married?" James asked.

"My father and hers worked together in business. Her father got his fortune from the railroad industry, hence having our own private train." He gestured toward the walls of the compartment.

"I imagine you were married young?"

"We were supposed to marry in October 1899, but she had an accident a few weeks before and eased her mind with a vacation abroad."

"You must've been worried," Martin said.

Alexander nodded. "Naturally, but I had faith in God that He would do what was best for her. For us. If it was her time to be with Him, then so be it."

"So be it? Why, it doesn't sound like you loved her at all. You didn't care if she died or not." Martin's voice grew in volume like a fire being kindled.

Alexander's mouth straightened into a thin line. "That's quite dramatic. Oh, Martin, you are a lost soul. We are but sheep to the Lord, our savior. Only He knows what is best for us."

"What was the nature of Fiona's accident?" James asked, refocusing the conversation.

"She never told me." He looked at his hands.

Martin raised a brow. "Never told you?"

"I'm afraid not. I focused on my work, that's what I do best. Luckily, Roger was there and took her to the hospital when she needed help. He said Fiona went to the hospital for the same thing three years prior, so it must not have been serious. They were close, but the fire that melded them together also sometimes burned them a part. I remember earlier that day they had a fight before she went to the hospital, but I supposed they worked it out. He was only too glad to pick her up later. I should've been there," Alexander added bitterly, "but I just couldn't see her in the state she was in. Roger told me she looked as white as a sheet. I couldn't have that be the last time I saw her in person." Alexander shook his head. "Not like this situation is any better. She was always so delicate, but her words were sharp and ragged. There is no wonder what she could have said to provoke such a response from her assailant. But alas, now she is at peace. God bless her." Alexander looked up to the crowned ceiling.

"At peace? She was murdered, you half-wit," Martin yelled.

Alexander snapped his head back to look at Martin. "What am I supposed to do about it, Mr. O'Reilly? Let passion drive me to my wit's end and blindly seek vengeance. I can see how that has scarred your soul. You're a fool. Nothing but a slave to your emotions." He closed his eyes. "Forgive me, for I forget what harm befell your wife. What twisted fate for her to have met and fallen for the likes of you."

James stood and pushed Martin out the door and into the hallway before it could escalate.

"Thanks for your cooperation," James added hurriedly.

"Pleasure," Alexander said, grinning.

James closed the door behind them. "Calm down. He is trying to cope with his loss in his own way."

Martin pushed James off him easily. "You're defending him?"

"Listen, we don't need another death on this trip." He walked down the corridor, his mind wandering off, trying to figure out how the conversation with Alexander fit among the others. He looked back to see Martin standing still and turned to face him.

"I don't care what anyone is going through, it doesn't give them the right to speak ill of me or my late wife. We may be working together, Anderson, but don't forget that while you know nothing about me, I know everything about you and that girl you let drown.

James's shoulders tensed. "It's okay to be angry, and I'm sorry for what he said back there. He just wants a response out of you, he's feeding off of it."

"I don't need a lecture. Certainly not from a cowardly policeman thrown out from his police station. You joined the force to 'save people' yet you couldn't save her. You were weak then and you're weak now."

James pushed Martin against the wall. "Don't drag my

life into this."

James felt his heart throb in his chest and closed his eyes. He felt his chest tighten and he knelt on the carpeted flooring. He put his head in his hands, letting the adrenaline race through his body like a drug. As Martin stood over him, his face fell like a wave crashing on the shore. He looked to either end of the hallway before bending over and pulling James back on his feet. The lights in the train dimmed for a moment before fixing themselves. James was quiet for a moment as he looked out at the inky sky through the window. When he finally turned to Martin, his face was solemn, like he had seen a ghost. "Come on, we have work to do."

Martin furrowed his brow, reevaluating the man beside him, then took out his notepad once more. He read through the pages. "Roger and Alexander seem to have a messy relationship. I would have dropped everything to support my wife, both at the hospital and after hearing about the row. Whatever fighting words are said to her, those are words for me to hear as well."

James shook his head. "He said it himself—he didn't love Fiona. She was just his business partner. What do you think they would have to argue about, Fiona and Roger?"

"Money issues, probably. Alexander said Roger needed cash. Perhaps Roger thought he'd have better luck getting money from Fiona than his brother," Martin said.

"It's possible. I suppose it depends on what the money is for. Then again, this crime was passionate. If Roger loved her as much as he's shown us, perhaps Fiona had thought of ending the affair or being with someone else." James looked off again in thought. "How about the fact that Alexander knew about Roger and Fiona's affair."

"It seems like Fiona was close to Roger before she married Alexander," Martin stated.

James nodded. "We need to know what Fiona was in the hospital for. If anyone knows what it was about, it would be him."

Martin shoved the notepad back into his pocket. "We can ask about it tomorrow."

"We don't have till tomorrow. We will be in North Conway soon."

"And thank goodness for that." Martin laughed half-heartedly. "We still have time. Besides, the police can help when we get to North Conway. And this story will be the front page of the news, I can guarantee that."

"It better not be!"

The voice boomed from behind them. They turned around to see Roger coming toward them.

"We can't deny the public the truth," Martin said.

"What 'truth' have you boys dug up?" Roger sneered, his eyes suspicious. "James, I trust you to keep this out of the papers. Keep your friend Martin on a tight leash." He turned to Martin. "Why can't people find other things to stick their noses in."

Martin chuckled. "People like living vicariously through the rich and famous. There's a truth for you."

"I have to say, this trip will dampen my enthusiasm for any future endeavors on this train, you must agree with me there. Perhaps the drink will lighten the ambiance. Let me show you some hospitality by offering it to you both. I always like to drink some red wine before bed anyways." Roger gestured behind him toward his room.

James nodded, feeling a new weight on his chest as he thought of what he was going to ask Roger first.

"Why not," Martin said. "However, red wine is an acquired taste. Scotch is more fitting."

"At this time of night?" Roger shrugged. "I might have a bottle or two stored away."

# Chapter Ten

Roger pulled out his key and whisked the two men through his door, then lumbered through it and made his way to the other side of the room, picking up one of the two bottles that stood underneath his liquor trolley. "I'm afraid to say it will have to be served as is. I don't want to bother Dean at this time."

Martin walked over to Roger and held out his hand to inspect the bottle, which Roger reluctantly handed to him. Martin's fingertips followed the gold etchings near the top of the bottle. The label detailed that it was a limited edition of the 1896 Taylor Fladgate Old Tawny Port.

"Where did you get this?" he asked.

Roger gestured for the return of the bottle and caressed the glass, his hand drifting toward the neck that held the engraving. "I had it sent from the Douro region of Portugal. It's a very sweet wine. Fiona's favorite from when we went back in 1896. Since then, I've always had a bottle for her at the ready."

"You and Fiona traveled to Portugal together in 1896?" James asked, raising his brow toward Martin, who immediately took out his notebook. Roger watched the interaction between the two.

"Yes. We wanted to travel the world together. Yet, responsibilities and loyalties change and fade into broken promises," he added bitterly.

Martin scratched the back of his head with the pencil. "Did you travel anywhere else besides Portugal, or was that the only time you were able to travel with her?"

"None of it matters anymore. Let's get on with the drink, for we have all had a long day."

Martin pocketed the notebook and walked toward Roger after the small pop of the wine bottle. James looked around the room, picture frames facedown on the table and empty wine glasses scattered about. "Roger?" he ventured. "How is your relationship with Alexander?"

Roger mumbled, diligently pouring the wine into the last few crystal glasses that stood like soldiers on the tray. "Oh, fine. We live together, we work together. Nothing out of the ordinary."

Martin took a drink off the tray as Roger finished pouring the first glass. He filled another two and handed one to James.

James nodded in appreciation upon receiving the drink. "He doesn't get under your skin at all?"

"Well, of course he does. But it's nothing to sneeze at." Roger looked up to find Martin pouring the rest of the bottle into his empty glass. "Enjoyed the wine?" Roger remarked, tightening his jaw. He tightly held the stem of his glass and sat on the couch, gesturing for James to sit with him.

James planted himself across from Roger. "How about when you were cut from your mother's will?"

Roger snorted. "Ah, you heard about that. Yes, my mother was upset with me. She always was. But when you have a 'perfect' brother to compete with, it's hardly a fight worth having."

"Why were you cut from the will?" James watched as Roger doggedly finished his drink.

"It's complicated. I made a bet with my father before he passed, and I won." Roger swirled the red liquor in his glass.

"What kind of bet?" James asked.

"It was his idea. You see, I had originally asked my father to lend me some money. He agreed, but you must understand that my father was a gambling man. He struck a deal with me that if I won this bet, I wouldn't have to pay him back. On other hand, if I lost—" Roger stopped himself to see James stare at him expectantly. He sighed. "If I lost, I would leave our family and never come back."

James shook his head. "Those are abnormally high stakes."

Roger shrugged. "He was the one who proposed it. Besides, I needed the money, and I knew I would win."

"What was this bet?"

"I was to take an old saloon in New Hampshire, The Old Salt Box, and make it a success. On paper, I had to triple their earnings in the first year. And I did. I put my blood and sweat into that place. I rebranded the place Hexate, after Hecate, the Greek goddess of magic and spells."

"That still doesn't explain why you were cut from the will," Martin interjected, looking up from his glass to walk over and sit next to James. "Being here now, we can safely assume you won and therefore are still a part of the family."

"My father didn't expect me to win. He thought this was a way for me to be detached from the family for good. He wanted me to pay him back for Hexate, which I adamantly refused. It wasn't until he threatened to have me arrested that I relented. When my mother found out about what I'd bargained for, I was taken out of the will. To her, family was everything." He paused in reflection. "If you think about it, my father ended up winning after all."

"And you were able to afford it, paying back your father?" James asked.

"Everything comes at a cost. I found a way to give my father what he was due, no more, no less."

Martin changed the topic. "We found a note the other day and discovered a name. We were told you might know who this person is."

Roger kept his eyes on his wine as it swayed back and forth in his hand. "Well, what is it?"

"Selene," Martin said, in little more than a whisper.

Roger's hand stilled, the red current settling itself in the curve of his glass. His face turned to stone. "Selene? I can't say we've had a Selene in our midst for quite some time. Some time indeed. Probably one of Fiona's family members. You know, you could ask Clara about it." He scratched his head and tried to smile, yet his eyes darted back and forth. "I do apologize that you two found such a disturbing note." Roger looked between Martin and James as he spoke.

"It's part of the job. If anything, it is a string to sew this mystery together." James paused. "Hang on. No one said the note was disturbing." He watched Roger fidget with his hands.

"Oh, I just put two and two together. You found it just lying around, you say? God, man. I should fire the maid at once."

James took a sip of his wine. "That won't be necessary."

Roger steadied himself and leaned back into the

couch, crossing one leg over the other as he regained his composure. "Probably for the best not to. I don't think Alexander would have it anyway. He doesn't like change in the slightest, though I like to think I can keep him on his toes. Can't have him getting fat and lazy on me." He smiled and took a sip of his drink.

"I didn't think he'd be the type." James chuckled.

"He's an old dog, Alexander. Not that I really mind. He likes being unaware of what's going on, it's a trait that runs in the family. Naivety can only get you so far, I say. The world is changing, and we must change with it. If I were Fiona, I would've gone insane."

"What is it about Alexander that bothers you?" James asked.

"Alexander keeps living the high life, thinking he is untouchable and immortal. Sometimes it seems like he created his own little world away from all of us. His own reality." Roger shook his head. "And I don't blame him half the time, but again, the world is changing, and he must change with it."

"And Fiona, was she not bothered by this attitude as much as you are?"

"I presume not. Though, she wasn't pleased to find out she was going to marry him. It was unnatural, but our mothers had to have everything their way."

"Why is that?" Martin asked.

Roger flicked his glass with the side of his thumb. "She was a wicked woman, my mother. I didn't agree with her half of the time, and she thought Fiona wasn't a 'good fit' for me. Yet, Fiona was just perfect for Alexander."

"Why was Fiona not a good fit for you?" James followed, feeling his eyelids begin to droop. He wondered what time it was.

"I don't give a damn." Roger pounded his palm onto

the table he sat at, causing James to sit up a little straighter. A couple of moments passed before he looked back at James and Martin.

"I'm dreadfully sorry. With everything going on, there has been a lot on my mind."

"I understand. It seems like Fiona meant a great deal to you." James stood and walked toward Roger's desk, hoping the movement would help keep him awake.

Roger cleared his throat. "More than you could ever know."

"How did you meet?" Martin asked.

Roger finished his drink and put his glass down. "We were friends, met at an art gallery when we were sixteen. Then our fathers went into business together. My mother saw the promise in Fiona—it was fruitless to deny her beauty, intelligence, and kind heart. But I was the spare, and my mother cared more about establishing my brother, her favorite, the eldest." Roger paused. "I suppose that's not entirely fair. You see, our family's fortune was dwindling and my mother in her old ways thought that marrying Fiona would guarantee our legacy." He spat at the word. "Legacy," he muttered. "As if there aren't more important things in the world."

"Was maintaining a legacy important to Fiona?" James asked.

Roger rubbed his eyebrow. "It was always hard to tell with her what she thought of everything. She kept quiet about her thoughts. Her position made her more trapped than I was. She always tried to see the best in everyone, even my brother, which has led to her downfall. I hope she knew that she could rely on me. I did everything to make sure she was safe."

"Why wouldn't she be safe?" James asked.

"Oh, I don't know. I just wanted her to feel comfortable. That's all."

Martin turned over a page in his book. "Alexander mentioned that Fiona was delicate. Do you know what he might have meant by it?"

"Ridiculous. What would he know? It wasn't like he was around very much."

Martin and James watched as Roger left his seat to open the other bottle of wine.

"Was Fiona happy being with him?" James asked.

"I don't know how interesting a life with Alexander as a husband could be. Luckily, she had me." Roger rested the cool glass against his forearm and broke the seal of the bottle.

"Alexander said you helped Fiona when she went to the hospital," James said.

"And that you had a row with her earlier," Martin added.

"Alexander has you all up in a knot," Roger snapped. "Yes, it was quite unfortunate, but she had a similar incident three years before. She was fine. Her wedding was pushed back until August." Roger sighed. "And it was hardly a row between us." He poured the alcohol in his glass and took the bottle with him to his seat, eyeing Martin.

James swirled the wine in his glass. "Why did she go to the hospital in the first place? Alexander didn't fill in all the gaps."

"Those are her private medical records. I can't discuss that with you."

"It would be better to know what happened now. If you don't tell us, we will just request her papers when we get to town," Martin persisted.

Roger wrung his hands. "She would have these panic episodes. Get flush in the face and hollering."

"What were you fighting about that night before she went to the hospital? You say now that she had these panic episodes, but then why were you arguing if you knew she could react this way?" James asked.

"She was impossible sometimes, inconsolable. Stubborn as Hell."

"What was it you discussed before the hospital; it must have been important," Martin reiterated.

Roger hesitated for a second before slouching his shoulders. "Isn't it obvious? She didn't want to marry Alexander, but no one cared. She didn't want to lie anymore. I didn't want to lie anymore."

"Why would that create such a heated debate between the two of you if you wanted the same thing?" James asked.

"She was afraid to do anything about it. Afraid of change, perhaps. I suppose that is how she was like Alexander. Even the other night, she refused to have any talk of leaving him." Roger clenched his fist. "I was always the one there for her, not him. He was never good enough for her."

"Then who would be? You said it yourself: no man is perfect, not even you," Martin said.

Roger's eyes flashed toward Martin as he finished his glass of wine in one go, but he didn't say a word.

James walked closer to Roger. "Your history with Fiona makes me wonder if something happened between you two the night she was murdered. Could her hesitance in leaving him cause you to act out your frustration? You loved her, didn't you? And even after her marriage with Alexander, you never stopped loving her. Did she refuse you when you came to her that night, when you asked her to be with you instead?"

Roger lunged toward James, knocking over everything on the small table, and struck the side of James's head. Martin tore the man off James, who felt the thick wetness of blood trail the side of his head. Roger tried to shake Martin's grip, which only made Martin hold on tighter as he escorted him to his seat. Roger wiped a glob of saliva that was trailing down his rounded chin.

"My God, man, pull yourself together," Martin mumbled, waiting until Roger had recomposed himself before letting go of the back of Roger's shirt. Roger's brown eyes softened as he looked at the shattered picture frame that had fallen off the small table before him, as if he had been awoken from a dream.

James walked over to the frame and picked it up. He saw a black and white photo of a young woman who had long hair neatly tucked behind her right ear, a small ring on her finger, and bright eyes. As different as she looked in the picture, so full of life and promise, it was unmistakably Fiona. James picked through the glass to take out the photo and turned it over to read the inscription. "All my love forever, Fiona."

Looking back at Roger, James saw his shoulders tighten as his gaze fell to the floor. James moved next to Martin and held the picture out to Roger. Roger took the photo and held it against his chest.

James breathed in deeply and used the edge of his hand to wipe the blood from his head. "Listen, I want to find out what happened to Fiona. You might've loved her at one point—Hell, you might love her still—but I need to know about your full relationship with her from start to finish. Both the good"—James pointed to the picture— "and the bad." James noticed a used cloth napkin and picked it up to stop the blood from moving down his face. He walked over and fell back into the chair across from Roger. "We have to find out what happened to her. For her sake. Don't you want that, too?"

"Of course, I do," Roger mumbled, lifting his eyes off the floor. He looked at Martin with a pained expression before turning to look at James.

"I never hit her. Let me make that very clear. I could never hurt her, no matter what she said to me." His voice cracked. "I loved her, and she kept telling me that one day we would be together. Run away from the pressures of society and be whoever we wanted to be. When we were sixteen, I knew I wanted to marry her. I brought her home to my family, and she was measured up to be the bride of my brother. I went to Alexander and told him how much she meant to me. But that night I found out our brotherhood was nothing to the evils of society, to the legacy he thought as a firstborn he had to uphold. She loved me; I know she did. We were together for six years until her marriage, and together we suffered through heartache and loss. It was the October before her wedding to Alexander that she told me she was pregnant with our child. The wedding got pushed back, and Fiona and I went to England to hide the pregnancy until she gave birth— July 12th. Her lady's maid persuaded her to put our unborn child up for adoption. Adoption! I wasn't good enough to be her husband or a father to her child."

James didn't know what to say at first.

"What happened to this child?" Martin asked, piecing together the narrative.

"I assumed you've gathered that Clara was Fiona's lady's maid. Clara offered to set everything up for us for our daughter. I can only hope she is having a good life, wherever she is. I used to try to write to her, but after not getting any response, I gave up. I told Clara whenever she wants to know who her parents are or if she ever needs anything, I would be there. That's the least I could do. I always hoped that we could be a proper family, but I can't do it without Fiona."

Roger stood up and walked to his liquor cart, his back to Martin and James. He shuddered as he reached to grab the corners of the cart, seeing his reflection in the silver. "How the Hell did my life get to this point? Nothing matters anymore."

"What was the name of this girl?" Martin asked. "Maybe you can find her."

James looked to Martin and then back to Roger. "Her name was Selene, wasn't it?"

Roger nodded. "That was the name Fiona gave to our little girl when she was born." Roger stopped himself abruptly, memories flooding his mind. "Still, I wonder, what does she look like? What does she sound like? Maybe one day I'll have the privilege to know." Roger's voice trailed off into a whisper.

"Roger," Martin began, "we have reason to believe Selene is…" He trailed off, looking at James for help.

James shook his head, watching as Roger closed his eyes. Martin continued to stare at him expectantly.

James sighed. "I'm really sorry to have to be the one to tell you, but we have reason to believe she's no longer with us."

Roger sat back on the couch and smiled thinly. "No, I know she's still out there. She's fine. She's a Cross after all."

Martin cleared his throat. "But, sir, on the note we found—"

"Not everything written down on paper is the truth, Mr. O'Reilly." His voice flared as he opened his eyes. "When are you newspaper folk going to get this out of your system? You're bloodhounds, all of you. I'm sick and tired of worrying what the press will say. Who gives a damn. Miserable fools, like you, who have nothing better to do with their lives than document the issues of others." Roger closed his eyes. "Please leave. I want to be alone."

# Chapter Eleven

James and Martin left Roger to his thoughts. James's long strides caused Martin to take an extra step to catch up with him as they reached the dining room. Elizabeth and Clara were sitting at the bar, their hands wrapped around cocktail glasses filled with a red liquor and a few cherries lying across the rims of the glasses on toothpicks—Manhattans.

Upon seeing James and Martin, Clara stood. "Good heavens. I should get cleaned up for bed. Martin, dear, there is something we have to discuss first." Clara straightened her skirt while James turned to Martin, who looked just as confused as he was. Clara looped her arm through Martin's and whisked him away.

James pushed himself onto the chair Clara had left open next to Elizabeth. She slowly ate the three cherries from her drink, licking her lips before placing the toothpick beside the glass.

"How are you?" Elizabeth began.

"Alright, I suppose. And you?"

"Exceptionally bored." Elizabeth smiled, breaking her eye contact with James.

"How could you possibly be bored? You're free to do whatever you'd like," James said, a hint of jealousy in his voice.

She laughed. "Freedom is a silly word. Is it too hasty to presume the individual you were so keen on talking to is me? Truly, I am quite honored our famous detective has time to speak with me given there's a murderer lurking about."

James watched as Elizabeth tucked a strand of hair behind her ear. "Your work with the Cross family does make you someone of interest."

"Your work in this entire affair makes you someone of interest, James. You better be careful, before you get taken out next." She began to twirl the charms on her bracelet, which became entangled on her wrist. "Silly things, always get stuck." After separating the rubies and diamonds from the brass charms of keys, dragonflies, and a few moons, Elizabeth noticed James's interest. "This was a gift from my father. He bought it for me on my birthday many years ago, only now can I wear it properly. My mother—if I can call her that—would never let me wear it in public. She believed young girls were not supposed to wear jewelry this precious."

"Are you close with her, your mother?"

Elizabeth's face darkened. "Money ruined any chance at that. It consumed her, and she did everything she could to get more of it. Listen, I'm glad this is where our discussion is headed, because I need to talk to you. Seems like you're the only one who will listen."

James raised a brow. He heard the clinking of glasses and turned to find Dean emerging from the kitchen with freshly washed glasses, a fresh lemon scent trailing behind him as he entered the bar and began putting the glasses away.

Elizabeth paid him no mind. "I'm worried." Her face was stoic as she took another sip from her drink. "About Alex," she added. "The Cross family has a lot of enemies, even among themselves. From what I've known of Fiona, the little I did, she was wrapped up in a lot of problems that were not her own doing."

"What problems?"

"Alexander told me she was having an affair. Being the Christian that he is, I'm sure he has told you everything by now. Nonetheless, he refused to divorce her. He said he needed her for something, and Fiona never left him. I begged him to leave her. He deserved so much better, to be with someone who truly loved him. I don't understand how he can find it in his heart to forgive her, or his brother. He has done everything for them."

"Why are you telling me this now?"

"I don't know." She looked into her glass. "I'm angry with everyone, especially Fiona. God, it sounds awful to say aloud. But isn't her undoing her own fault?"

"Her fault she was murdered? No, I don't believe anyone should decide who lives and who doesn't."

Elizabeth gripped her drink and groaned. "You're sounding like Alex again." She got to her feet, finishing the liquor in her glass.

James stood after her. "Do you know what Clara wanted to talk to Martin about?"

She cocked her head. "Haven't a clue, but my goodness it is getting quite late. You better save Martin from Clara; he must be bored out of his mind. I will find you for breakfast, perhaps then you can enlighten me on their conversation. It is nice to finally have someone to talk to who can match my wit." Her white teeth shined brilliantly under the lights as she smiled. "Until then."

Once Elizabeth had left, James turned back toward the bar, letting the silence sink in.

"You don't have much time left."

James looked over to the only person left in the room, Dean, who was hunched over behind the bar as he cleaned by the sink. His hand went back and forth like a metronome as he cleaned the silver meticulously. His shaggy hair fell into his face.

"What do you mean?" James asked.

Dean pushed his hair from his eyes. "A caipirinha? I haven't made one of those in a while, so I'll have to check the back to see if we have extra limes." Dean quickly looked left and right, then tilted his head toward the kitchen for James to follow.

Once James entered the small room, Dean closed the large wooden door behind them and locked it. While his back was turned to James, he began to speak.

"I only started working for Roger a year ago. Hired as a part-time bartender for Roger's place Hexate. He said I could make a little extra cash if I worked on this train as a server."

"That's a lot of work to do by yourself." James looked behind him and found a large carton to sit on.

Dean shrugged, his unruly long hair sticking to the sweat around his hairline. "I couldn't turn it down. A man has to do what a man has to do. It's how the rich get to subjugate working men like us. We're all just puppets and they're our puppet masters. If you know what I mean." He pushed himself next to James and pulled out a dark yellow ROLL-O box of cigarettes. "Want one?"

"No thanks, I quit a couple of years ago." James tried to air out his shirt as the room grew hotter.

"Are you sure?" Dean laughed, yet his eyes grew serious as he watched James look around the room. He pushed the box into James's hand and watched as he opened the flap. On the thin cardboard box, the small design of a moon was printed.

"Just one hit, I think, would do a snooper like you some good," Dean said, reaching over to take a cigarette out of the box James held. "Or are you chicken?"

James looked at the white, playful font on the box and laughed. "I don't need to prove anything to you."

"Good. You're cut from a different cloth, Anderson. You're not like the rest of 'em." Dean snatched the cigarette box back and put it into his pocket, his pants a size too big.

"That's the best compliment I've gotten in a while," James jested, fixing the cuffs of his shirtsleeves.

Dean dropped the cigarette he'd started and ground it apart under his shoe. "I knew one of 'em would die, it was only a matter of time. They have a lot of dirty laundry." He spoke slowly, pronouncing every syllable with bitterness. "But I heard that no one would get hurt until after we left the train."

James forced a laugh as he looked around the room. "Who have you been listening to?"

Dean gave him a hard look. "It's easier for someone like me to hear things they're not supposed to. It doesn't matter now, not to us, and not to them."

"What doesn't matter?"

"Her death. Fiona. No one gives a damn about anyone unless they give them something in return." Dean snorted. "You have to stop thinking so highly of people."

James rolled his eyes. "Can we save the discussion, if that is what this is, for later? What is your purpose for bringing me here at this hour?"

"Don't be so ignorant. Someone had to have known this would happen. Where it would happen. When. Not everyone here is good."

"Not everyone here is bad, and I'm trying to root out what is going on here. Now if you don't have any further insights." James stood, reaching for the doorknob.

Dean put his hand out to stop him. "Speaking to them hasn't changed your mind? If they were all good, we wouldn't be facing this issue, now would we?" Dean spat into the corner. "These people are sending you on a wild goose chase, playing you like a deck of cards. You really think Clara or Elizabeth care about Fiona? To them it's just drama. What about Martin? He gets a sizzling story to advance his career. Then you have Alexander and Roger, who both profit from her death. To them, people die every day, what's another one?"

James scanned the man glowering at him. "To someone, Fiona meant everything to them. You say not everyone is good, but not everyone is bad. You think people plan on being 'bad?' What does that even mean? Most people only want to make ends meet or make up for something that shouldn't have ever happened in the first place."

"Who are you, James Anderson? You stand there and judge, thinking you're some kind of God. Trying to figure each of us out."

"I don't pretend to be more than I am. I only want to find out who killed Fiona and why."

"Stop trying to be the hero!"

"Relax," James said, furrowing his brow as he reevaluated this intense man.

Dean whistled while reaching for a match in his pocket. With a snap, the flame erupted over the small scrap of wood. He looked the flame over, letting it grow in volume as it luminously skated over his fingertips. "We all are monsters, Anderson. Some are just worse than others."

"Do you include yourself in this statement? The real question here, Dean, is who are *you*? Why do you care so much about these people you freely work for?"

"I'm your ally. Probably the only one you have here besides that boob Martin." He quenched the flame from the match between his fingers. "I know everything about these people: their habits, their desires, their secrets. Who is to say I'm not next? I can't fall asleep without thinking it. Just another working-class man who could be tossed in the street and forgotten."

"What did you bring me in here for? Protection?" James asked.

Dean nodded toward the cigarette box. "Pick it up."

James grabbed the cigarette box from the floor and handed it to him. Dean rotated the yellow box to the side that had the drawing of the moon. His fingernails dug into the celestial box.

"It's a crescent moon, the symbol of the Greek Titan Goddess of the moon."

"Just because it is a crescent moon does not associate it with a Greek Titan or have any relevance."

"Do you know of any cigarette companies that use this design?"

"No."

"Exactly. James, you have to look at this case from a completely different angle than the one you've been on. You've been looking at the bare minimum of everything that has happened. You can talk to people and hear their words, but what are they really saying?"

"I think you may have had a little too much of this stuff, that's what I'm saying."

Dean pushed his face closer to James's. "Look into my eyes. Do my pupils look dilated?"

"Now that you mention it," James jested.

"Be serious. Now stop asking the dumb, boring questions. Look at this box. What do you see?" Dean shoved the box into James's hands and pointed at it.

"A white and blue crescent moon on a yellow box, with silver lace etched into the corners."

"And what do you know about the moon?"

"The moon goes through phases."

"Good, keep going."

"There are eight phases of the moon."

"Yes. Now, remember how you are the extra on the train, correct? The one who wasn't planning to be aboard. How many people besides you and the conductor started on the train?"

"You, Martin, Clara, Fiona, Elizabeth, Alexander, Roger, and Ruth. Eight." James thought for a moment. "But surely that is coincidental."

Dean raised an eyebrow. "Is it?" He reached into his pocket and pulled out a picture. "Go on, give it a look." His demeanor was cold as he callously threw it toward James.

James picked it up and held it toward the light. The square illuminated into a ripped picture of a young girl standing outside a small house beside the lake. "What is this picture?"

"It's of Selene. I found it in Roger's desk when I was working at Hexate."

"How did you know it was her?" James asked.

Dean sat down on the carton and gestured for James to sit next him. He opened the cigarette box and took out a cigarette. "I knew Selene a long time ago. I need you to find her for me. I have to save her from him." He rolled up his sleeve, unveiling a small sun and moon tattoo underneath his forearm. "I know this is a lot to take in, but we don't have much time left." He rolled down his sleeve and leaned against the wall. "You see, it was just the two of us for a while. The farmer and his wife couldn't have children of her own. We lived in some old farmhouse, 15 Continental, I think it was." Dean snorted with disgust. "I hung in there for a while, until I got a job at fourteen working on the railroads. Once the war came, I lied about my age and was conscripted to go over to France. I thought I'd never see Selene again and got this tattoo in honor of her. I loved her and would have done anything for her. When I returned from the war, Selene was gone. I asked my mother where I'd find Selene, and she told me Clara would know. I knew Clara wouldn't recognize me, so I wrote her a note asking her about Selene, and I got this." Dean shoved his hand into his pocket and took out a battered note.

*Selene is lost*

"I've carried it with me this entire time. Everyone seemed to have forgotten her, everyone except me." Dean leaned his head back against the wall. "I want to know what happened to her, the truth that Clara isn't willing to share."

"You seem to know a lot about Greek mythology," James said, staring at the note.

Dean shrugged. "My dad's friend taught me about mythology. I don't really remember him, but he practically breathed mythology. Uncle Fred, we used to call him. Of course, he wasn't really our uncle, just a parent's close friend. He would tell us these stories of Titans and Gods when he came over. It made us always look forward to seeing him."

James stood silently, his lips pursed.

Dean rolled his sleeve up again to reveal his tattoo of a sun. "It makes sense, doesn't it? An all-seeing God being the server to all these socialites, being the only one to see who they really are." He let out a laugh as he gripped the tattooed skin. "Botched tattoo, isn't it? My buddy Marius did it, said he was an artist. Should've asked him to draw for me first."

James tried to smile, but it drooped into a frown. "What regiment were you placed in?"

"I was a farrier for the 106th regiment, a striker at the time. Yours?"

"United States Army Coast Artillery Corps."

Dean put a cigarette up to his dry lips. "Hard to believe it's been, what, over six years." His eyes wandered to the crates around him. "But I'd never want to go back to the way things were before the war. Not for me anyway. I just wish I could know what happened to Selene. I know she is not lost. That's why you must help me find her before she ends up dead or something."

James was quiet, watching the desperation flood his eyes.

"That Clara woman is a liar. When I went home after the war, I wanted to know where I came from. My adoptive parents on the farm told me everything I needed to know. Poor Selene. I wonder who she became." He spat again, revealing the thick yellow tobacco stains against his teeth.

"What makes you so worried about her," James asked. "Couldn't she have left to find a better path, like you did?"

Dean shook her head. "She wasn't like me. She was the

golden child and did whatever needed to be done to help the family."

"Like what?"

Dean grimaced, as if the thought repulsed him. "There was one man who paid each month to visit us. I was uncomfortable with him and would keep myself in the bathroom. Yet she stayed, uncomplaining, as he watched her. He didn't care for me."

James furrowed his brow. "Who was this man?"

"I always called him the tall man. Always dressed in black with tall hats. But one month he stopped coming. When we lost that income, that was the hardest of times." He cracked the knuckles in his hand, each one popping rhythmically.

"Did you ever find out why he stopped coming?"

"No, my parents never found out why. You should ask that wretched woman, she would know."

"Who?" James asked.

"Clara of course. She knew everything about Selene, and I bet my bottom dollar that she did something. Now, I can't be a part of this. I must keep this job. I have to stay on the sidelines. Do you understand?"

"You don't get a choice—"

The sound of a bell echoed into the room. "That's my cue." Dean stood, brushing the dust of the room off his pants. "Could you grab that crate of silver? In case anyone asks," he explained.

James shrugged and pulled the crate off the shelf, then followed Dean out of the pantry. Walking past him, he placed the silver on top of the bar. His eyes strayed to the bell to see who was ringing. "I thought you went to sleep."

Elizabeth stood in a long white nightgown. A pair of white, silk gloves adorned her hands. "I did, but I need to ask Dean for some help."

James turned to Dean, who looked like he had seen a ghost.

"Dean, are you alright?" James went behind the bar to pour the man a glass of water. Dean shook his head, like he was struggling to wake up from a nightmare. James pushed the water into his hands.

Dean corrected his expression, returning a pacified stare. "Of course, Miss Kingston. How may I assist?"

"Do you have an extra canister of Pond's Cold Cream in the back? I seemed to have run out."

"Of course, miss." Dean whisked through the doors to find the extra canister.

"Can you deliver it to my room?" she called after him. "I'll be waiting for you."

Elizabeth turned to James and looked him up and down. "Isn't it past your bedtime, detective?"

James ignored the comment. "Can you have Dean come find me once he's returned?"

"You're worried he won't come back?" Elizabeth twirled a wisp of hair around her finger suggestively. "I'll make sure he is still here when you wake up, honey, don't worry. Who knows what was happening in that pantry, hmm?" She winked before turning on her heel.

James looked down at his watch before begrudgingly walking back to his compartment. He eyed the intricate weave of the carpet as his feet dragged across it. Arriving at his door, he unlocked it and entered. James looked around his compartment, making sure *Alice's Adventures in Wonderland* was right where he left it. He picked up the book delicately, as if he was holding the world in his hands. His fingers slid over the brown cloth cover and he flipped through the pages. Scrawled handwriting filled the margins beside the fine print, and the scent of the paper and coffee rose from the page. When he'd left North Conway, he hadn't wanted to bring anything to remind him of Anne. It was only a week later when a parcel containing the book arrived at the front door of his apartment in New York.

As he sat, his mind grew weary, his eyelids slowly drooping over his eyes.

# Chapter Twelve

When James woke up the next morning, his neck felt like it was made from wood. He stretched his back, trying to revitalize his muscles. As he rubbed his aching neck from where it had lolled in the night, he caught motion of someone running past his door. In his wrinkled clothes from the previous night, he peered out the door to see Clara running down the hallway, her skirt brushing against the walls. His curiosity getting the better of him, James hurried to follow behind.

"Clara?" he called, without a response. James quickened his pace. "Clara!" He projected his voice louder. She stopped, and James rubbed his eye as he caught up to her.

"Clara, what's the matter?" James held back a yawn.

"I thought detectives knew everything," Clara jested, letting the wrinkled corners of her mouth turn upward. "I didn't want to bother anyone, but I have a migraine and was looking for some medication. I suppose I should give up on my adventure and ask the maid." Clara paused. "I'll be fine. Shoo." She gestured, her hands pushing him away.

"While we're both here, would you mind if we had a quick word?" he asked.

Clara crossed her arms. "What part about having a migraine do you not understand? Besides, I thought we had discussed everything during our last little chat."

"It won't take long, I promise." He straightened his shirt as Clara scrutinized him.

"Not more than ten minutes. I suppose I would rather get this over with than have to deal with you later." She tucked her hair behind her ear. "Let's get going then."

"We can speak in my compartment; it's closer," he proposed, wanting to get it over with as well.

Clara's lips curled into a snarl. "Certainly not. That will hardly be adequate. My compartment is more suitable."

James shrugged. The two of them walked toward Clara's room, with Clara slightly bumping into James every few steps. "Sorry about that, dear," Clara said upon colliding with James like a bowling ball rolling into the gutter.

"Here we are." James watched as Clara fished for her key to open the door, but it was already unlocked. "I must have forgotten to lock it. I could have sworn I did." She rubbed her temple as she walked into the room, picking up her shawl from the desk chair and throwing it around her shoulders. She walked to the golden cushions facing away from the window, the light making the chair look like the sun. James closed the door behind them.

Clara sighed. "Let's get on with it."

"It's about the child you put up for adoption. How did she die?" James asked.

Clara shifted uncomfortably. "Getting right to it then."

She placed the fringe of her shawl between her fingers, her eyes focused on her hand. "My friend told me one day when Selene was three, she was playing with her imaginary friends outside and must've run off and got lost. We never found her, so she was presumed dead."

"You said before that she died of pneumonia. What is it?" James said bitterly.

"I believe she must have died from pneumonia; she did run away in January."

"That doesn't make sense. Why would she run away in the winter?"

"How the Devil would I know. She was a wild child."

"Why would you continue to ask Roger for money to support his daughter when you thought she was dead? You could have at least told him she ran away."

"You have no idea what you're talking about. Roger would have killed me for losing his daughter. I did them a service by giving them hope Selene was doing well." Clara slouched. "In the beginning, I gave all the money from Roger and Fiona to Selene's adoptive family. However, Roger wasn't paying me anything after I was forced to leave my position with them. I asked for support, but he turned me away. When my husband sprained his back and was out of work—" She cut herself off. "You must understand. We had so little money, I had to do whatever I could to make ends meet. I gave the family less and less as the months went by, as I needed the money to support Fred and me. He became addicted to his opioids, drink, and gambling and was a shell of the man I had once loved." Clara straightened her back. "I'm not proud of what I've done, but the Cross family goes back for generations and wealth is not something they lack," she added in resentment.

"I'm sorry about your husband." James took a seat beside Clara.

Clara rolled her eyes. "No, you're not. Continue please. Let's finish your questions."

"Did you know Roger was cut from his mother's will? What would you have done if he couldn't pay? Would you turn to Fiona instead to cash in on their secret? Is it possible that once Fiona went to bed, you slipped in to confront her about the affair?"

"That would never be a problem. I think deep down Roger knew that paying me was the right thing to do. Child or no child. He'd find the money." Clara let out a hollow laugh. "You're going about this all wrong. It's obvious if I do say so myself. Elizabeth worked with Alexander and started to fall in love with him. She started from nothing. He has always been her way out of poverty, so she murdered Fiona to be with him." Clara smiled as she pulled up the edges of her sleeves. "This murder is clear cut, James, do not overthink it. I'm sure they will appreciate your work when we get to North Conway. Another case of passion and love gone wrong. I may have blackmailed Roger, but it was to continue his hope that Selene was alive and well. It was for his own good, even if he didn't see it that way."

"It's pretty serious to accuse someone of murder. What makes you so sure?"

"Oh pish, it's the same thing you do in your line of work, is it not? Pointing fingers. You're just getting upset because you know I'm right." Clara smiled. "I, at least, gave Roger and Fiona the chance to hide their affair. Whoever did this wanted it to be seen. People don't harm one another without reason. We are not savages. Yet maybe things should have remained old-fashioned, like the Vikings. An eye for an eye. Perhaps that is what they're going for. I loved Fiona, but having that child set off a catastrophe in its wake, and I hated her for it."

James's brow furrowed as he sorted the information.

Clara shook her head. "You must not come from a big family. If that were the case, you would have a better understanding of being able to both love and despise another." She stood, adjusting her dress. "Then again, what is a family? Whatever this is, is not one. Not in the right sense."

'What do you mean?"

"You know exactly what I mean. You probably grew up with loving and supportive parents, who treasured you above all else. You don't know what it was like for those children abandoned by their parents and left with a big, gaping hole in their hearts for the rest of their lives. I had to watch them grow, struggle to figure out who they are. Watch them fall like the Cross Estate that will be torn down when the money runs out. Family is everything, and a broken family is what created this utter chaos. A cracked foundation."

"I know what that loss feels like." James rubbed his forefinger against his thumb's cuticle. "Those children? What are you talking about?" Clara turned to look out the window, pulling the shawl tightly around her. James jumped at the sound of a knock on the door. Clara eyed him as she walked across the room. When Clara swung the door open, Elizabeth was leaning against the doorframe nonchalantly.

"Here you two are. You're going to miss breakfast. I helped plan a lovely spread for our last morning together. We have toast, hard boiled eggs, and jam. I also found some more of my Mon Coeur tea for you both to try." She looked past Clara. "James, are you a tea drinker? I can't recall. Either way, I will have a pot made for us."

"We will be there soon," James replied hurriedly.

Clara tightened her shawl around her shoulders. "Come on, James, we can't let our hosts wait for us. Besides, you owe them a meal after missing dinner last night." She didn't wait for a response as she followed Elizabeth to the dining coach.

James's head was spinning. This new discovery of another child filled any want for food and drink, as he pondered why no one mentioned another, not even Roger. Perhaps the other one wasn't his, for why would he pursue one but not the other. James looked up at the sound of a knock against the doorframe.

"You look like you're in a rough state, pal." Martin lit a cigarette and then shook out the match.

"I was just going to find you. There is another child. I think this is more than just the case of a missing girl."

"No kidding," Martin answered in cool fascination. He had slept well. "Come on, let's get some food in you. You must be starving on nothing but apple pie from last night."

"This news doesn't concern you?" James asked.

"Of course it does. But the present has more pressing matters. You're as pale as a ghost."

"I've been in worse states."

"Perk up, buttercup." Martin walked into the room and slung his arm around James. The toxins from the cigarette rose to his face.

James pushed Martin off as they walked to the dining coach. All members of the family were seated, taking a crack at their eggs with their spoons. The sun gleamed through the crystalware and created miniature rainbows throughout the coach. Martin threw his cigarette into a glass of water in front of him, then pulled out the chair next to Roger. James took the seat between Roger and Elizabeth, watching as Clara kept looking from her egg to him. She finished her cup of tea, placed the china on its saucer, and promptly left the room. Elizabeth followed her out of the room as the men enjoyed their breakfast. It was only a moment later that she returned.

"What a lovely day we're having," Alexander began, filling the void.

Elizabeth ignored him and tugged on James's arm as she sat down. "What do you think of the tea?" She refused to make eye contact as she poured one for herself.

James looked at the cup of tea, already delicately poured for him on a saucer and doily. He smiled. "I'm looking forward to trying it."

"Why didn't I get any?" Martin huffed, jealousy etched onto his face.

She shrugged. "I didn't think you'd appreciate it as much as James."

Martin took the teacup from James's saucer and lifted it to his lips, taking a large sip. "What is in it?"

"Just a little something for the nerves. I know from the bags under his eyes James hasn't been sleeping well."

"Is it that obvious?" James replied lightheartedly.

"Eat, James. God knows you will need strength to deal with this horrible business when we get to the station," Alexander said, watching as Roger stood and left the room.

"He doesn't need you patronizing him, Alex," Elizabeth said, repositioning her napkin over her lap. "Who do you have waiting for you at home? Is there anyone who can take care of you?"

"Don't worry about me," James said, cracking the egg with his spoon. "I manage just fine on my own."

"No girlfriend, no wife?" Elizabeth placed her hand on James's knee under the table, letting her eyes finally meet his.

"It's complicated," James responded, pushing her hand off him, harsher than he intended.

She recoiled and positioned herself closer to Alexander.

"Do tell," Alexander prodded, slathering raspberry jam onto toast.

"You don't want to hear about it." James's heart rate accelerated, memories flooding his mind. The water, the blood, the branding. He felt lightheaded as his body began to twitch, suddenly feeling out of focus. He gripped his hands together in his lap and closed his eyes, trying to stop the convulsions buzzing through his nerves. Hating how weak and exposed this reaction made him. When he opened his eyes, the three were looking at him, puzzled.

Martin whistled. "Golly, you must tell us after that spectacle."

"I'd prefer not to, thank you very much." James bit the inside of his cheek, moving a hand up to his arm to hold himself together.

Martin laughed. "I didn't know you were so dramatic." He looked James up and down. "Perhaps I should have interviewed you instead of Elizabeth."

Elizabeth pouted and opened her mouth to say something, but quickly changed her mind. She looked to James, her eyes softening.

"There is no need to focus on James. Martin, why don't you tell us the story of your wife," Alexander said casually. He looked up to see Martin's face fall, relishing it. He smiled eerily. "Out with it then."

James watched as Martin's face grew a crimson color. "Forget it, Martin. Come on, there have to be more suitable things to talk about over breakfast."

"No. I will tell you exactly what happened." Martin

took another sip of the tea that was laid out in front of James. "I'm not a chicken."

Elizabeth's eyes darkened. "Oh, please don't bore us. We know your story. It was written in black and white in the paper. You must have some nasty friends considering the paper you work for was the very one to pin up your dirty laundry." She smirked. "How embarrassing."

Martin smiled a desolate smile. "Isn't it ironic that my story was one I was not allowed to tell? If you were smart enough, you would have noticed that I was not the author of that story; those were not my words."

Alexander stood, the table shaking from the abrupt force. "I will not have you insulting Elizabeth. I don't care if I'm doing this for Chief Michaels, I will drop you out the window if I must." Alexander reached for another slice of toast before sitting down.

"Elizabeth can hold her own. She's made that very clear." James crossed his arms. He leaned back into his chair to slow down his heart rate, his arms still jerking every few seconds.

Martin wiped his mouth with the back of his sleeve and stood up, as if he was preaching his case. "I'm in debt. Not the kind you can just pay off and forget about, either." He whipped his head to look at James. "I've ruined lives from what I did. You get deeper and deeper in dealings like that and you're doomed. I'm doomed, James. I thought I was in control, but I was just getting used by people in high places." Everything you've ever seen me write in the paper is half-truths, and that's the way it'll always have to be. I can't say what I want, not anymore." He glared at Alexander. "Your family would know all about that, wouldn't they?"

Alexander snorted. "I don't know what you're talking about."

James reevaluated his partner. "What happened to you?"

Martin put his hand out, silencing James. "No one can help me now. I'm dealing with the Devil."

There was a moment of silence.

James sighed. "What did you *do*? What can be so bad that it hangs over your head like this?"

Martin wrung his hands. "It started with small things. Writing slander in the paper: accusing people of bank robberies, illegal gambling, fake jewelry. I was told the names and spun a web around them."

"Small things?" James scoffed. "Why did you do this? Who made you do it?"

"I needed the money to provide for my wife. We lived in a small house on the outskirts of the city but being a journalist didn't get me the income I needed."

"Of course. A man not taking responsibility for his actions and instead blaming a woman. What else is new?" Elizabeth said bitterly.

Martin turned to Elizabeth. "My wife had no idea what I was doing. I told her I got a raise and was working extra shifts to explain the jump in funds." He turned back to James. "When my wife told me she was pregnant, I didn't want to have any more part in the crimes. The money wasn't worth it anymore. I wanted to be there for my child. I told the gang I didn't want to be involved anymore. As you can imagine, that didn't go over well, and I was worried they would come after me, or worse, my wife. It made sense in a twisted way for them to silence me, as I knew more about their operations and plans than anyone. That's how I met Chief Michaels. I reported everything to him, and the gang leader was caught. We both paid the price in prison, as I confessed my crime, and

I thought that would be the end of it. I was foolish to think so." Martin sat down again next to James.

James shifted his weight and leaned in to listen.

Martin slouched his shoulders, as if he could feel the weight from his tale taking a physical toll. "When I was in prison, she had our baby boy; I found out from my older brother, Jim. He told me she named him Edward, and he was a happy, healthy baby. I was released from the Elmira Reformatory on September 15th, 1922—early, for good behavior. I didn't tell anyone except for a buddy of mine, who I asked for a ride home. I wanted to surprise Margie, my wife. But as we approached my neighborhood—the fire was everywhere."

He looked over at Alexander, who remained unfazed.

"For the first time in my life, I prayed. The car didn't properly stop before I tore open the door and raced down the street, stumbling as dread built up in my gut. My pal came after me and held me back when I found that it was my house that was burning. I screamed, calling out for her, but there was only silence. I tried desperately to run into the house, but my pal kept me back as the roof collapsed in on itself. I fell to my knees—the heat against my skin felt as if the Devil was spitting in my face. Most nights, I wish I'd been killed rather than live with this guilt for the rest of my life. It's my fault they're dead. I know it is." Martin tried to lean back in his chair, heat coursing through his body from the anger and passion that welled inside of him.

James didn't know what to say at first, and from the stares of Alexander and Elizabeth, they didn't know how to begin either.

Suddenly, Dean stumbled into the dining car, blood dripping down his pristine uniform.

"Clara. Has been. Killed." He put his hand over his

chest, trying to catch his breath, then pushed his way into the pantry and came out with towels and water.

"Where is she?" James called out to Dean.

"She's in her room."

"Come on," Martin said, relieved to have ended the conversation pitiless.

He ran to the scene with James, Elizabeth, and Alexander on his heels. They looked through the open doorway of Clara's room to find Roger with Clara sprawled out before him. Her face was pale, the color drained from her body. The incandescent lights in the compartment reflected off a blade that Roger held in his hand. Blood on the letter opener ruined the silver and ruby visage that decorated the blade. Roger dropped the letter opener onto the floor and desperately looked up at James and Martin.

"I knew it," Martin gasped. "We will be in North Conway soon, and there you will be charged for the murders of Clara O'Donnell and Fiona Cross." Martin's voice grew as he walked toward Roger like a predator approaching his prey.

James gestured for Alexander and Elizabeth to stay outside, then walked into the room with Martin, grimacing at the pungent smell of iron.

"This isn't what it looks like. I had nothing to do with this," Roger pleaded. "I found her like this not a moment ago. I'd gone back to my room to change, and when I was walking back to the dining car, I heard a cry. Clara was sputtering for air and fumbling with her locket. I caught her as she fell. Next thing I knew, Dean was looking in the room and then ran off."

"You are a vile, evil, conniving man," Martin yelled.

"Martin, can we talk for a moment?" James asked.

Without waiting for a response, he grabbed the cuff of Martin's sleeve and pulled him outside the compartment.

"We can't be sure it's him." James paused, letting go of Martin's cuff.

"What the Hell are you saying? He has the murder weapon; he has had it the entire time." Martin seethed. "God's sake, man, this is an easy open and shut case. Don't make it more than it already is. He has been playing us. Lying to us left and right."

James ran a hand through his hair. "They've all been lying to us left and right. But let's face it, this was too coincidental."

"Too coincidental? We've been tearing this place apart since the murder began. This is our big break. Why are you making this difficult? Don't you want this case to be closed?"

"Not if that means accusing the wrong person. You have to put your feelings aside for a moment." James walked back into Clara's compartment with Martin trailing behind him. "Roger, please place the letter opener and the locket onto the vanity and step away from her."

Roger gently laid Clara's body on the floor, stood and brushed the carpet off his knees, then solemnly did what he was told. As he walked away from Clara, he looked at his hands and the blood that covered him, his lips pulling together in a grim line.

Hearing Elizabeth sobbing from the corridor, James poked his head outside to see Elizabeth turn her head away from the scene and press her body against Alexander for support. "Alexander, could you please escort Elizabeth back to her compartment. We will be talking to you both on the matter shortly," James added.

"What are we going to do with him?" Martin gestured toward Roger.

"We will have to hand him over to the police for questioning, as he was found at the crime scene."

Roger's face was like a marble bust, still and unfeeling. "After everything I've told you, you can't think it was me. I wanted you to investigate to find the killer, not accuse me."

Martin raised a brow. "You have to understand how this all looks, Roger. What else are we to think?"

"We're not accusing you outright, but we still have some unanswered questions. Please pack up your things for the station, we will be there soon."

They watched him leave.

Martin leaned his back against the wall of the compartment, looking down at the vanity that now held the murder weapon, the locket, and various kinds of makeup. "We're not going to have enough time to speak to each of them. We only have an hour left until we arrive at the station."

James picked up the letter opener, the year 1900 embossed under an engraved portrait of a young lady with her hair in ringlets. Only the right side of her face was shown, but the moon that crowned her head made it unique. James passed it to Martin. "I wonder if this is Selene, the Titaness."

"Has to be," Martin answered, fingering the knife. He placed it on the vanity and picked up the locket, wedging his nail between either side. "It won't open." He handed it to James.

James gave it a go before relenting. "Seems to be stuck." He eyed the scratches along the bottom of the locket before placing it into his pocket. "I know someone who can help us open it."

Martin picked up the letter opener again, turning it over in his hand. "Wouldn't be my first choice for a murder weapon."

"If that woman is Selene like we're supposing, the goal wasn't efficacy in this case."

James looked at the makeup that framed the vanity. It instantly took him back to the different colors and shades of makeup from when he had to organize the small apartment he shared with Anne. He looked at an opal jar, the lid just barely covering the top. It was a container of Pond's Cold Cream.

# Chapter Thirteen

James noticed the weight difference as soon as he picked up the jar. He twisted the lid the rest of the way off to find that the jar was empty, save for another note.

Martin was looking over his shoulder. "Roger has way too much free time on his hands to be sending us little notes. He's taunting us."

"We aren't sure of that yet. You must keep an open mind." James looked down at the paper. This one was text ripped out from the same kind of book as the other textual passages. "What is the reason for another note?" James asked, both to himself and to Martin. "We already completed the anagram."

"The Sun-God, enraged, darted forth infection on air, earth, and streams, and Syphilus became the first victim of the new disease," Martin read, scratching the small scruff on his chin. "None of the letters are underlined like the other notes."

"Why would the murderer spend their time writing about Syphilus? The other verses were from Homer about the abduction of Persephone by Hades. This is still Greek mythology but doesn't fit the general trend. Why Syphilis of all things?" James said. He looked back at Clara's body and tore down one of her curtains to drape on top of her, as they had done with Fiona.

"I can help with that."

James looked up to find Dean pulling his hands from his pockets as he walked over to hold the other side of the curtain. Together they lifted the curtain over her and let it cover her body.

"As a matter of fact, perhaps you could help us. We have a few questions about Greek mythology." James said.

Dean shook his head. "I told you before, I can't be involved in this in any way."

"This isn't about anything personal. You have nothing to worry about."

Dean looked at James uncomfortably. "Alright, shoot."

James picked up the letter opener. "Have you ever seen this before?" He showed Dean the blade.

"Never."

"Okay. Do you know who this woman on it could be?"

Dean held out his hand for James to hand him the letter opener. James placed it in his palm. "If I didn't know better, I would say this young girl could be anyone."

"And if you did know better?" Martin implored.

"Could be any deity associated with the moon. Hecate, Selene, Diana. Take your pick." Dean shrugged. "Mythology is confusing at the best of times."

James bit his cheek. "Alright, what do you know about the story of Syphilus."

"Syphilis? The disease?" Dean whispered, looking around to make sure no one heard.

"In Greek mythology, what was the explanation behind syphilis?" James asked.

Dean put his hands in his pockets again. "Well, there was a poem about it in a book series my Uncle Fred left hanging around. It was written by Girolamo Fracastoro. It was called *Syphilis sive morbus gallicus* — 'Syphilis or The French Disease.'"

"And?" Martin said.

"I'm getting there." Dean rolled his eyes. "It was about a young shepherd named Syphilius who looked after the flocks of King Alcinous. There was some sort of drought, and in response, Syphilius blasphemed Apollo and punished him with the disease. Later, the poem references that mercury or guaiaco was the cure." Dean looked between both men. "Can I get going now? I should be attending the other passengers. I'm sure they'll want a drink after what happened."

James stretched his back. "Of course."

Dean nodded before walking toward the dining car.

"By the way, Dean."

Dean reluctantly turned around. "What is it?"

"Was there an order for Pond's Cold Cream from Alexander?"

He furrowed his brow. "I have no idea what you're talking about. We weren't told to pick up anything."

"Thank you, that is all." James looked at the jar and straightened himself. "If you could be so kind as to lock this room for us, I would like to keep it secure for the time being."

Dean shrugged and pulled out a ring of keys. "I can lock up when you leave."

"Thank you." James and Martin closed the door behind them and watched as Dean locked the door.

Once Dean had left them, Martin turned to James. "What are you going on about orders?"

"Ruth mentioned they had to pick up an order of this

stuff for Elizabeth before they left New York. Was quite upset they had to do it." James walked down the corridor, where they found Ruth pushing a silver tea cart into Alexander's room.

"Ruth?"

The young woman looked back out into the hall. "Can't you see I'm busy?"

Martin put his hand up. "We just have a few questions for you."

"This better be good." She picked up a cloth that hung on her cart to wipe her hands.

James cleared his throat. "Before, you said Alexander had you pick up some of the Pond's Cold Cream for Elizabeth in case she ran out. We have been informed that Alexander made no such request."

She let out a laugh. "Typical for Alexander to say such a thing. Everyone knows why she needs the cream. What's the point in hiding it any longer?" She looked at Martin. "Maybe we've put this whole song and dance on just for you two."

"Why does she need the cream?" James asked.

"Ruth!" Alexander yelled. "Come here, now."

"I must be going." She looked down and traced the lines on her palm. "Ask Elizabeth to take off her gloves. That will give you all the information you need." Ruth put on a smile as she pushed her cart the rest of the way into Alexander's room.

Martin turned to James. "I hate this wild goose chase."

"Come on, we haven't much time." James pushed on to find Elizabeth, but as he took a step forward, he paused, turning to face Martin. "About earlier, with your wife and son—"

Martin pulled at his sleeve, his eyes fixated on the cuff. "It's my own fault for being naïve."

James placed his hand onto Martin's shoulder. "It isn't your fault. You're allowed to grieve and feel that loss."

Martin shrugged him off. "Let's go find Elizabeth."

James sighed and followed behind Martin to Elizabeth's compartment. They knocked on the door, but finding it unlocked, pushed it open.

"Elizabeth?" Martin said in a whisper.

"Y-Yes?" Her voice was unsteady.

"It's Martin and James, could we have a word?" Martin didn't wait for a response as he entered the compartment. Elizabeth was sitting on her lounge, her eyes a crimson red.

"Please leave me alone. I want to get off this train. I don't want to be next." Her body shook as if electricity jolted through her.

Martin went to her side and put his arm around her shoulders. "Hey, we're here. Anyone who messes with you is going to have to mess with us," he jested, watching her face sift through different, unreadable emotions.

She turned her head to allow her hair to splay down her back. She gave him the satisfaction of a small smile, and for the first time, she looked worn out. Like she had seen the horrors of the world.

Elizabeth looked up at James through her eyelashes. "What is it you came to see me about?"

"Well, we looked at the evidence in Clara's compartment and found a note in a Pond's Cold Cream jar. Since this cream was something you used often, perhaps you would understand why a note about syphilis was found in this jar, and any relevance it may have in our case."

Elizabeth's face turned a pasty white. "I never thought it could be her."

"Who?" asked Martin.

"Someone has been blackmailing me for years. I never

thought it was her. Why would she do this now? She could have asked if she needed money, or anything. I trusted her with my life." The shock on her face fizzled into something more sinister as a blooming anger flickered across her features.

James took a seat across from Elizabeth. "What has Clara been saying to you? Writing," he corrected himself.

Elizabeth looked from James to Martin, fear pooled in her eyes. "Nothing." She stood, her dress trailing behind her as she made her way to the door.

Martin reached for her wrist. "You must be brave. I told you my story, now you must trust us with yours."

She stood in the doorway, contemplating the consequences. "I should ask Alexander."

"He doesn't own you; you can say what you like."

Elizabeth shook her head. "No, no. I need him. He'll know what I should do."

James pointed to the pine trees that surrounded the car as they raced by. "We will be arriving soon. We need to know now. Why did Ruth tell us to have you take off your gloves?"

"That traitor," Elizabeth muttered, pulling at the fingertips of her gloves. When James and Martin didn't say anything in response, she continued. "If I tell you this, do I have your word that it won't be released in the press?" She looked from Martin to James.

"You have my word," James said.

Martin muttered in agreement.

Elizabeth sighed. "This entire process has taken over my life. I look into a mirror, and I can't recognize myself. I grew up poor. We didn't have much, but we had each other. We needed each other to survive. My father pressed on with the chores without any help, but after a particularly harsh winter, we ran out of money. I picked up a shift at a local bar; I can't remember the name now. But that was where I met Roger and Alexander. I sang on Thursday nights at first, and as I got popular, the more days I got to sing. My parents were thrilled and jumped at the opportunity I made for myself with Alexander. But no one understood the cost it was to get here." She paused, moving her left hand to stroke her right glove.

"What kind of cost?" Martin asked, fully immersed in the tale.

She shivered, the memory painful. "I was a prostitute at the bar when I was first hired. I needed the money, and when the bar manager refused to pay me an advance, I did what I had to do." Her eyes brimmed with tears. She looked at the ceiling to keep them in, but they disobeyed and ran down her cheek. She let them linger on her face as they accumulated in a steady stream.

"I first noticed something was off when I found that I had a single sore inside my mouth. It was ghastly, but undetectable and painless. I was relieved no one could see it. I didn't say anything out of embarrassment, and I couldn't afford to see a doctor. One of the other girls gave me mercury in a jar of Pond's Cold Cream. She said she cured her syphilis with it and kept the mercury in the jar so it would be unnoticeable. And it was. After the sore went away, I was relieved, if only temporarily."

"How does this relate to your gloves?" Martin asked.

Elizabeth gave him a glare before making eye contact with James. "A week later, I had a skin rash form on the palms of my hands." She pulled at each finger of her left glove meticulously before completely taking it off, revealing a spotted rash that adorned the palm of her hand. It was a rough, reddish-brown. "A couple of weeks ago, I began to feel very tired, and I had to cancel some shows. Alexander was furious, and after accusing me of sleeping around and getting drunk, I was forced to explain what was happening to him. Which brings me to why I'm really coming up to New Hampshire. I'm going to get the salvarsan injection to recover properly. I just hope it isn't too late."

"Why didn't you get it done in New York?" Martin asked. "I'm sure there are a lot of doctors there who could help."

"Too many people are watching my every move there. I thought it would be safer up here. I already sent the treatment kit to a doctor in Conway."

James looked closely at Elizabeth's hands and noticed a marking under her right wrist—the branding of a club. "When did you get that?"

"It was long ago. When I first started working at the saloon."

# Chapter Fourteen

At the sound of the train whistle, James shifted his attention from Elizabeth to the snow-filled fields that glided past them. The ringing of the bell indicated that they were slowing down, that the station was in sight. James walked over the window to admire the view, filing his thoughts. Elizabeth stood behind him, pulling her glove back on.

"Thank goodness we are getting off this forsaken train. I've certainly had my fill." Elizabeth gathered her things. "Now, you two must be gone."

James and Martin walked out of the compartment. James's compartment was the first they reached. Martin turned to James with his hand outstretched. "Don't know when I'll be seeing you again, pal, but this sure has been something."

James took his hand. "Oh, it's been something alright." He grinned.

As Martin continued to his own compartment, James repacked his suitcase, making a special spot for Anne's book safely surrounded by his clothes so it wouldn't get damaged. He felt a jolt as the train stopped and reached for the silver hook that adorned the wall to steady himself. He looked out the windows to watch the rolling steam seep from the large, black wheels of the train. James buttoned his navy coat and left his train key on the seat of his compartment, hoping that was the correct protocol.

"You can hand that to me," Dean said. He tilted his palm up to receive the key. James moved it from the seat to his hand. "Thank you." He grasped the key and moved it between his fingers, feeling the metal.

James nodded. "Hey, Dean, would you happen to know anything about stars in Greek mythology?"

Dean pushed the key into his pocket before leaning against the doorframe. "There was a lot of mythology surrounding stars. Do you mean if there was a God or Goddess who oversaw the stars, or like the origination story behind stars, or what the Greeks thought of constellations and stars?"

James sighed. "All this mythology is getting to my head. Never mind."

Dean was reluctant to leave with the question brewing in his head. "Some of the ancient Greeks saw the stars as unchanging and perfect. Constellations, or Katasterismoi, meant the "placings of the stars" and represented how the Greeks thought the Olympians put those people, animals, and objects in the heavens for the reason of being a lesson on proper behavior, sort of like the myths in general. Mind you, the stars, eclipses, and other celestial bodies had different meanings to different people. The ancients saw the stars as blest and divine guardians in some interpretations."

"Thanks, Dean. Where did you say you learned all of this?"

"My Uncle Fred started me on it. Since then, I read old books in Roger's library at his saloon. Helps pass the time."

"When do you have time for that?'

Dean smiled. "Don't you worry about me, James. I think the old man likes sharing his interest." He saluted James. "Best be off. I need to hand over the keys I gathered from everyone to Gerald."

"Could you make sure that everyone stays in the station until I can call for help?" James asked.

Dean was hesitant, "Not a problem."

Once Dean had departed, James walked through the corridors. It seemed like he was the last to get off. He stepped down the stairs of the train and reached the Conway station, which had been absorbed by the Boston and Maine Railroad in 1890. The stark air filled his lungs as he breathed it in, whispers of memories flooding his mind. He looked at the thin gray paneling that lined the walls of the building, large vertical windows on either side of the door that faced the platform. Dark metal collar beams attached from the sides of the station to the lower awning that provided shelter from snow, rain, or sun. The cider-colored awning swayed in the sunset, the wind carrying the small white waves that tapered over the side shook in the wind above a green sign that read **Conway.**

James looked back at the silver train that stood out against the glittering snow before gripping the handle of his suitcase and walking into the station. The area was small, lit by four lamps around the space. He proceeded to the main desk and was greeted by a man with shaggy dark hair and round green eyes, dirt crowning his hairline and shading his forehead.

"James?" The man stood from his chair, causing the floor to squeal as the chair was pushed back.

"Hey, Joe. Long time no see." James set his bag down as Joe unlocked the booth and hurried through.

"Long time no see? That's all I get after a year of not seeing you?" Joe punched his arm, a lopsided grin printed on his face. Joe had been James's best friend for years, but after a couple years in the police force, he decided to give it up and work with his father on the railway.

"We'll have to find time to catch up later, pal. I have to speak to Inspector Evans. Do you have a phone I could use?"

"Sure thing." Joe went back behind the desk to grab the phone. James took the phone in appreciation and stared at the dial. He removed the receiver, careful to not hit the switch hook. He pulled his fingers into a fist to warm them as he listened for the steady humming to indicate the line was ready to call. He put his forefinger into the dial and pulled it around until his finger touched the finger stop before releasing the spring to allow it to return to the normal position. He began with the number eight and allowed for the dial to return to its position before pulling the following numbers: one, nine, seven, zero. His heart raced as he waited for either the busy or ringing signal to begin and felt relieved with the intermittent burring sound of the bell of the other telephone ring.

James hunched over the phone as he waited for the Inspector to pick up. Joe tugged on his arm. "What?" James mouthed, fixing the receiver to his ear.

James followed Joe's line of sight to find a man entering the station. He was dressed in a charcoal button-down shirt with a button lost, revealing the collar of a white undershirt. He had a pin in the left breast of his shirt next to a starred badge. His hair was freshly cut close to his head, emphasizing his large, round ears. His lips were organized into a thin, unfeeling line. On the bridge of his crooked nose sat a pair of thick-rimmed glasses, his eyebrows fully visible over the glass. His hazel eyes were warm as they looked James up and down. The man adjusted his hat before continuing toward them.

James put down the receiver. "Inspector Evans, I —"

Evans clasped his hands around James's arms. "I'm glad you're back, son." He dropped his arms and turned to Joe. "A bet's a bet, Joe. I knew he would come."

Joe snorted. "Of course you did." He fished through his pocket and pulled out a quarter, tossing it to the Inspector.

"You bet on me not coming back?" James remarked, incredulous.

Evans shrugged. "Come on, James, it's just a bit of fun." He turned to Joe. "I'll close the station up. Run home to Jill; I'm sure she's already finished cooking something up."

Joe thanked Evans for closing as he grabbed his coat from the desk and left the station, gesturing goodbye. Once Joe was gone, James turned to Evans.

"We need to call for backup. There was a double homicide on the train."

"Good God, James!" Evans eyes widened as he looked about the station. "And all these people?"

James dragged his finger on the phone to pull the numbers to dial the medical examiner. "I've had everyone stay in the train station until I was able to get help."

"Call for backup next. We need to close the train. Has it left the station?"

The rotund conductor was sitting on the bench and stood up to walk over to the Inspector. "She is still sitting in the cold, not that it'll do any good to her." He paused. "The name is Gerald, Inspector."

Evans nodded, "Alright, Gerald. Make sure no one goes into the train until Dr. Lewis arrives. It will likely remain locked in the station until we sort out this mess."

"On it, sir." Gerald mumbled as he walked toward the windows facing the train and looked out to keep watch.

James put down the phone. "Lewis will be here in a minute."

"Good." Evans received a tap on his shoulder blade.

"Excuse me, Inspector. This is rather silly of me, but did I hear you correctly when you said that the train is to be locked in the station?" Alexander asked.

"That's right, sir. We can't have the train depart until we've finished with our investigation."

Alexander's face soured before he recovered his charm. "You have to agree that this is rather ridiculous."

"I'm sorry sir. It's just the protocol in homicide investigations." Evans raised his brow.

Alexander gestured towards Elizabeth. "You have to understand that we have a celebrity on board. Elizabeth Kingston. Perhaps you've heard of her?" We must be going, you of all people must understand?"

"Even if she was the president of the United States, we cannot risk the train leaving and corrupting any evidence." Evans remained firm.

"But what of Elizabeth's tour? At the very least she has an appointment that would be very costly to rearrange. Money that perhaps could serve you better?"

"There is no need to be hasty, sir. We will not be keeping you all overnight, Elizabeth will have no problem going to her appointment. Is there someone you can call to pick you up from this cold? I'm sure James can arrange for someone to get you if need be."

Alexander snorted before he walked over to James. "Don't worry, James. I have friends in all areas of work."

James handed Alexander the base of the phone before making his way next to Evans, who was watching Dr. Lewis's park his car.

"Who was that delightful man?" Evans asked quietly, turning to James.

"Alexander Cross." James then nodded to each of the other members of the family in the station and informed Evans of their name and connection to Alexander.

"Wonderful." Evans said, clapping his hands together. "Well let us split up and get their contact information before Alexander's friend comes to get them. I'll take those on the left and you can on the right."

James agreed before finding Elizabeth on the right. Her ankles neatly tucked under her on the green cushioned bench. Roger had his arm over her shoulders, he was speaking to her in a hushed manner. Her bright eyes connected with James as the squeaky wooden flooring announced his presence. Elizabeth abruptly stood, Roger's arm falling off her. She tucked her hair behind her ear as she tried to pass James.

"Are you alright?" He asked. Knowing how dumb of a question that was to ask at a time like this. Elizabeth looked around and closed her eyes, letting out a thin smile. "Of course. Why would anything be wrong?" She held her hands in front of her dress. Her voice coming out a little more than a whisper. "Two women dead on a train. It's madness. First Fiona, and now Clara? What am I to do with myself? I'm next, I swear it! I feel exhausted but this animalistic fear is burning back my eyelids." She turned to Alexander, "This is all your fault!"

Evans was speaking with Dr. Lewis, who had just arrived, when the accusation was put into place. He looked at James and tilted his head.

"Why is this Alexander's fault?" James asked.

"I don't feel like talking about it. But if he didn't make us go on this stupid train then none of this would've happened. But now everything's changed, hasn't it?"

"It's okay to be uneasy. This is a very traumatic experience for everyone." James said. If you ever don't feel safe you can always call either Evans or I, or any of us from our department to help you. It's what we're here for. We want to help."

"Where were you when Clara was killed? Let's face it, sweetheart. You're reactive, not proactive."

"Where are you going to be these next few weeks? In case anything else arises and we need to speak again?" James asked.

"Close by, I reckon. Alexander and Roger still have to sort their grandmother's assets with the coroner. Now Fiona's as well. Then we will be going to Portland for my tour."

"Alexander said you have an appointment soon?"

"Oh yes, I forgot about that. It's in two days at an address here in Conway. I don't remember it, but Alexander knows. He arranged it."

"Thank you. Again, if you need anything, please don't hesitate to find me."

Elizabeth relaxed her shoulders and looked back at Alexander, who had moved to lean against the wall next to Dean.

"Anderson?" Dr. Lewis was thin and lanky, with eyes a deep blue and wavy dark hair framing his face. He put out his hand, "It's good to see you again. Honest. I hope you didn't lose yourself down in New York?"

James shrugged, "Still in one piece."

Lewis nodded. "I wish we reconvened under better circumstances, but I suppose I expected little less from you." His lips turned into a grin. The same one that James remembered when they met at camp. Lewis shook his demeanor. "Evans said he would finish with collecting contact for the rest of the group. Can you take me into the train to where the bodies are?"

"Certainly." James beckoned Lewis to follow him as they went by the station door. "Gerald, can you open the doors for us."

"If I must." Gerald muttered as he pulled his jacket together and went outside.

James put his hands into his pockets as he felt the harsh wind sting his eyes, looking back to make sure Lewis was still behind him as they approached the train. After Gerald opened the doors, he turned to James as they went in.

"I don't think I can ever ride this train again." Gerald took the keys out of his pocket while Lewis followed behind the two men. The bright colors that brought life into the train now looked muted. Perhaps what brought life to this place was the people. But like this place, those people had changed.

"I don't blame you," Lewis said as they stopped in front of Fiona's compartment. "Luckily the walls have ears, and we will sort out this mess in no time. Isn't that right, James?"

James nodded as Gerald opened the door. "If that will be all, I'm going to help Evans with the report.

Lewis furrowed his brow as he looked down at James. "And James if you ever need anything. You're not alone." He let out a smile before hitting James's arm, "My offer still stands if you need someplace to live."

"In that haunted house of yours, I think I'll pass." James teased.

Lewis grinned. "I'll take care of everything here. I have a feeling we will see each other soon enough."

James nodded before exiting the train and heading

back towards the station, a few men in uniform passing him to get on the train.

The members onboard *The Blue Star* had left when James got to the station, leaving Evans alone on the bench with his thoughts. "Backup came right after you left. Went by quickly. A few men went to help Lewis with the bodies."

"Good. Is there anything else that needs to be done?"

Evans stood and put his hand on his shoulder. "There is nothing left for us to do until the morning. Let's get going before Rose gets too worried." Evans tossed him the car keys. "You remember how to drive the Ford, right?"

"Yes, sir." James clutched the key and felt his fingernails dig into the palm of his hand.

"Call me Evans. You don't work for me anymore. Now come on, we have much to discuss."

"You have no idea," James replied.

James slid onto the beat-up leather seat as he had done so many times before and shifted the car into gear before igniting the engine. As the low-riding car hit every rock and pebble along Main Street, James's mind couldn't help but wander in nostalgia at his childhood home. The familiar sight of Christmas lights adorning every building, along with small evergreen wreaths dressed in red ribbons bigger than their own good, calmed him down as he raced through the streets.

"For some reason, I don't remember your driving being this terrible," Evans said.

James could feel Evans's smile as they raced past Florence Silverstein's Jewelry store on the corner. "I don't remember you being so sarcastic," James said, stealing a glance at Evans.

Evans's jet-black hair had glints of silver along the nape of his neck, and his eyes highlighted the crow's-feet that spread from the corners of his eyes.

"Keep your eyes on the road. How many times do I have to tell you?"

James knew his way around town better than anyone, as if it was drawn on the back of his hand.

When they gained speed, Evans yelled, "Slow down, James. You're not in New York anymore."

"I'm sorry, sir. A lot on my mind."

"Hmm." His expression shifted to concern as he turned to face the road. "As I said, you have no reason to address me as sir. You don't work for me anymore."

"That's up for debate, seeing as I dropped everything to be here."

"You didn't have to come."

James shrugged. "I had no choice."

Evans pulled a pipe out of his jacket as he adjusted his position on the beat-up seat. "What happened on the train?" Evans inquired, bringing the pipe to his mouth, the wooden piece hanging off his scarred lip like an ornament on a Christmas tree. Without answering, James pulled into Evans's driveway. "Park her here tonight. You'll be staying with me for a while. We have an extra room, and it'll be nice for the Mrs."

James pulled the key out of the ignition and opened his car door. His mind raced with familiarity as his shoes flattened the snow beneath him. He looked to the naked oak tree that matched the height of the white colonial home, its limbs scratching the red brick chimney and thin gray slates that made up the roof. Snow bundled around the house, as if tucking a blanket around the base. The front door was a sanguine red, stark against the many windows that faced the front, like multiple pairs of eyes.

The curtain that closed the lid of one of the bottom eyes fluttered, and James heard the door unlock.

Mrs. Evans—Rose as she told James to call her—was tying the front of her jacket as she stepped down the few steps and onto the snow. Inspector Evans shot James a look that he recognized—behave and don't cause a fuss.

While Evans was more of a complicated knot, his better half was the hot iron that smoothed out his wrinkles. Rose was beaming as she made her way toward them, her small slippers kicking up the dusting of snow. She put her hands in front of her before cupping James's face.

"James. Why, it's so nice to see you." She let go of his face to evaluate him. "Still not eating much. You're stick thin." She placed the back of her hand against his stomach lightly. "Where is the meat on those bones?" Rose put her hands on her hips in disapproval. "It's good you're here, let me make you something to eat." Her hawk eyes turned to her husband. "Bring him in, no dawdling. I'll whip something up quick for the both of you."

"Ah, Rose, let the boy rest," Evans said.

She shot him a look before walking back to the house. James smiled as he walked through the door, feeling the heat from the fireplace as Evans closed the door behind them. When he entered, he gripped the handrail of the dark wooden staircase that wound its way upstairs. As he untied his shoes, he looked into the library. Filled with red and golden tomes, that room was always his favorite. James just finished untying his first shoe when he heard nails running against the wooden planked flooring. He took off his other shoe as a small Cavalier King Charles Spaniel ran up to him.

"Winston." He smiled while he scratched Winston's ears. Evans watched as Winston stuck out his long pink tongue in appreciation.

"He's missed you."

Winston rubbed his face against James's leg, brown gunk from his eye staining his pants. Evans picked up Winston. "Sorry about that. We can't seem to figure out why he does it. If you leave your pants in the bathroom, I can ask Rose to try to get it out for you while you're gone tomorrow."

James furrowed his brow. "What's tomorrow?"

"Let's go into the library to talk it all over." Evans pushed the library door the rest of the way open and beckoned James through it.

"Where are you taking him, he just got here?" Rose called out from the kitchen.

"Don't you worry," Evans yelled back. "Just in the library."

The only response from Rose was the sound of the stove clicking on.

Evans grunted as he walked over to a plush red chair and sat. "Now, what do we have here about a murder on *The Blue Star*? I like to do a hard cross off when it comes to investigations like this one. Let's start at the beginning." Evans took a puff from his pipe.

James left the room to grab his suitcase, opening it in front of Evans as he took out the evidence he'd gathered on the train. He went over the interactions with Roger, Clara, Alexander, Dean, Ruth, and Elizabeth, as well as the notes and Greek mythology references. Once he had finished, he fell back onto the blue and white plaid chair that was across from Evans.

Evans scratched his head. "I can't believe you let that journalist work with you."

"That's the first thing you say?" James said incredulously. "After all that."

"He can't be trusted. If everything we know is printed it's going to make this case harder than it needs to be."

"What do you think about Fiona and Clara?"

Evans waited to respond as Rose knocked.

"Food is ready."

"Thank you, we'll be there soon."

"You better be." The wood floor creaked as she went upstairs.

Evans looked off in thought. "Tricky. They all have complicated personal lives, but who has motive to kill both Clara and Fiona? That is the key. And, James, it's all in front of you. What you've gathered is enough to arrest Roger. He was angry Clara manipulated Fiona to put the baby up for adoption and didn't let him see her, and frustrated with Fiona for not leaving Alexander to be with him. Also because she did not see Roger as good enough to be a father to Selene. You said Roger studied Greek mythology, so of course he is leaving those notes."

"But he loved Fiona. I could see him possibly murdering Clara, but it's much harder to believe he would ever harm Fiona. He was the one who wanted me to keep investigating her case."

"Some murderers like the attention. But to be sure, I will need to get back onto the train to further investigate. *The Blue Star* will be closed until further notice. And James? Don't do any more investigating into this. It's better for both our sakes. Keep your nose clean. It's bad enough you got wrapped up into this."

James felt the sting rise onto his cheeks. "I didn't mean to get involved."

"Trouble always seems to have a firm grasp on you. Hand me all of the evidence you've gathered and I'll bring it in. You may not be bound to our protocol anymore, but your involvement can't be overlooked."

"I know." James handed Evans the ring, necklace, and notes he had been given. "But I can help on this one. I was there."

"Honestly, James, you have to open your eyes. It's the same reason why you couldn't investigate Anne's case; you were a suspect in Anne's case and now you're a suspect in this one. I thought the move to New York would clear the fog from your mind. We have to solve these crimes according to the laws and regulations. I hope to not hear of you straying from those laws like you did with Anne's case, or it will be curtains for you. You hear me? Curtains," he emphasized.

"You should be grateful I was there. I was able to understand possible motives. Besides, everything that happened before I left is in the past. I'm fine."

Evans shot up out of his chair. "Are you? Do not get yourself any more involved. It's for your own good. You're not ready for this."

"I couldn't just sit back and do nothing." James turned to look out the ice-laden window, calming his anger. Feeling the buzzing of his nerves kick up again, he tried to quell the thoughts of her.

Evans stared at James's back. "Quit being selfish. You weren't the only one affected when Anne passed."

James was quiet for a moment before turning to face Evans. "This is why I left in the first place."

"Don't give me that attitude. You're not leaving yet. You have work to do." Evans opened a drawer next to his seat and pulled out an envelope. He walked over and hit James in the chest with it.

James wrapped his hands around the envelope, squinting to deceiver the messy handwriting as his heart raced. Once the blurry lines resolved into English, James looked up at the inspector, his emotions roiling like the sea. "This is the letter from my father?" He took a deep breath, "He doesn't even have the decency to see me in person."

"Just read the damn letter," Evans said.

James snorted, feeling the top of the envelope already split open. "You read it."

"Of course I did." The inspector shrugged. "Had to make sure it was actually him this time. I wouldn't have called you for no reason."

"If you say so." James eyed Evans, bending the envelope in his hands. "If he really wants to speak to me, you can tell him to find me here." He positioned his hands to rip the envelope in half.

"You are just like your father." Evans sat back down.

James's face reddened, aglow against the fire, he now hesitated to rip the envelope.

"Caiden wants to meet you outside Chelsea's for lunch tomorrow, at half past eleven," Evans said, impatience flooding him.

James felt a knot in his stomach. It had been nearly ten years since he last saw his father. "You're not coming?"

Flames crackled in the fireplace, reflecting in Evans's eyes. "You were right about Anne's case. I need you to help me find out what happened to her, to work with Caiden and figure out what is going on."

James furrowed his brow. "How do we know Caiden has any clue what he's doing?"

Evans pulled on his pipe. "Your father may not always have his head on straight, but he was always good at picking up on clues. We don't have a choice, James. We have to trust him. If there is any chance to find out what happened to Anne, we must take it."

"Why do you need me? Couldn't Caiden just speak to you about it?"

"His sole condition to investigating her case was to speak with you first. In person," the inspector said.

James was silent as he looked around the room. Admiring the rows of books and the photos of Anne that adorned the shelves. He nodded, watching as Evans sighed back into his chair. For the first time, James thought he looked old. Gray hair rested on top of his head like smoke, only trickling down into some parts of his hairline. Purple crescent moons hung underneath his eyes from restless sleep, the eyes themselves pools of loss, the fire extinguished from them long ago.

The floorboards announced Rose's arrival from the kitchen. She carried a green and white checkered hand towel, which she hit James with lightly on the back of his arm. "What about dinner? You've let the food go to waste." She looked from James to her husband, who had closed his eyes. "Come on, do I have to do everything around here?"

James obediently followed her into the kitchen and sat on a wicker chair, watching as Rose relit the stove with a match before putting the soup pan over the flame once more.

"You mustn't mind him. He hasn't been doing well since he lost both of you." She let the match die in the air before lifting the brown triangular top of the small trash can to throw it away.

"I'm sorry," James said.

She pinched his cheek. "Come now. You don't need to apologize to me. I will always love you." As she let go of his face, her own fell. "Promise me one thing."

James nodded, his heart heavy in his chest.

She turned to the stove and took off the soup, pouring it into a bowl. "Be smart. I can't lose you too." She handed him the bowl and kissed his cheek. "I'll set up Anne's room for you upstairs. I just finished the laundry this afternoon." She looked back at him one last time before disappearing up the stairs.

"Thank you," he called after her. "I'll be up soon."

After James finished his soup, he stood from the dark oak table to wash the dish and placed it in the sink. His eyes glazed over with familiarity as he left the kitchen and entered the living room, which looked the same as he remembered it.

In the middle of the room was a gray couch beside a small table with a glass of red wine, a novel sprawled across the cushion. The corner of the room housed a wooden tea cart with twin porcelain dolls sitting on top. He looked at the wall to find the same collection of butter plates next to antique spoons and a glass green wine pourer. The scent of vanilla breezed through the room as he walked across the braided rug. He heard Evans stomp upstairs, the floorboards groaning under his weight. James walked toward the stairs and put his palm on the handrail, tracing a long, spiraling scratch from when Anne was carrying her skis downstairs for the fresh winter snow a couple of years back.

Hushed whispers floated down the staircase.

"I will not have him staying in her room. Give him the spare bedroom, that's what it's for," Evans whispered.

"Don't be ridiculous. I just washed her sheets; the spare bedroom linens are dirty."

"It is just for a few nights. He will be fine."

"He is our guest, and we have a perfectly good bedroom that is ready and not being used."

James reached the top of the stairs.

Evans looked James over. "You know what's best," he said to his wife. He pulled out his pipe from his pocket and moved closer to James. He put his hand on James's shoulder and squeezed it before walking past his wife back downstairs.

Rose nodded to James as she walked into Anne's room, turning on a small tableside lamp. The walls were a cream color with a floral design of red roses and lavender intertwined. There were two tall vertical windows parallel to one another draped with a crimson curtain tied back to either side. James watched as Rose put the pink sheets onto the mattress, then helped her place the duvet over the top. She pulled back the blankets religiously and looked about the room.

"If you need anything, you can help yourself." She winked, trying to lighten the mood. "Is this okay? Charlie said it may be hard for you to be in here. But I figured it may give you some comfort."

James was quiet as his eyes went from the rocking chair to the bed, then to Rose. "This is fine, no need to fuss over me." He forced a smile as she turned and began to close the door.

"I brought up your suitcase. It's by the dresser."

"Thank you," James replied, seeing his case tucked to the right of the white dresser.

Once the door was closed, he walked to the dresser to unpack his suitcase. As he reached down, he noticed a stack of letters beside the brass candlestick on top of the dresser. He picked up the pile. The sharp edge of the letter pricked his thumb as he read it over, recognizing the black handwriting as his own. His fingers went to the incision in the envelope, and he pulled out the note he had written. His eyes gravitated toward the date on the upper right-hand corner: June 25th.

~

# The Solar Eclipse

June 25th

*My Dearest,*

*Meet me at our usual spot tomorrow by Echo Lake at seven. I wouldn't miss a chance to see you for the world.*

*Love always,*

*J*


Memory from that fateful day flooded his mind.

# Chapter Fifteen

It was supposed to be the best day of my life, not the worst.

It was just another Tuesday. That's what I wanted her to think.

Anne would be out of work at five, which gave me approximately two hours to get ready. I looked into the long mirror to straighten my white button-up shirt and tuck it into my pants, wrapping a black belt around my waist. I combed my hair; it was longer then, more carefree. That's who we were, Anne and I—carefree. I turned to the dresser top to put my wallet into my pocket and stared at the small blue box next to it. It was silly, really. To be nervous for such a thing. Anne and I had been together since high school. She didn't get the best grades in school, adhere to the dress code, or follow her curfew, but she was perfect to me. Anne was the anchor against my turbulent sea. I grinned, thinking about her. Let that warmth fill me. While I was never sure where I wanted to end up, I knew I wanted her to be by my side. I think that's when you know you've found your soulmate—

when you know that as long as you're with them, everything is going to be okay.

The summer wind pushed against me as I stepped outside, causing the thin fabric of my shirt to billow out. I straightened my bike from the side of the house and pushed it forward with one leg before hiking the other over onto the pedal. I cycled faster and faster, letting the fresh scents fill my lungs. The sticky, sweet smell of strawberries surrounded me. A small red cart was selling fresh jam and eggs on the corner. When I reached the bend, the trees towered over me, providing shade from the summer heat. My heart raced with the exertion, and my cheeks began to hurt from the smile that was smeared across my face. Pine and lilac filled my lungs as I raced through the woods. Sprouts of wild purple irises stood in rows as I pushed through the trail to our usual meeting place at Cathedral Ledge on the Echo Lake Trail.

I'd told Anne to meet me there after her shift at the five-and-dime. It was just a few miles off Main Street, but it was enough to get away from everything for a moment. We'd first hiked this trail many years ago. She had brought Winston, a puppy at the time, his short legs bounding over rock and uneven ground, a green harness wrapped around his small frame. He had fallen into a gopher's hole, and we took turns carrying him. It was midday when we finally took a break on a flat rock at the peak of the mountain. We sat on the ledge looking over the hills and lake together, and that was when she first said she loved me. And I said that I loved her back. That feels like ages ago, and I suppose in some ways it is.

When I reached our spot that day in June, I sat down on that same rock. Swinging my legs over the edge, I thought of her. The scent of roses that follows her when she walks, her grace and kindness that was in everything she did. Her auburn hair crowning her midnight blue eyes, and her smile, which made you feel like you were her entire world. I reached into my pocket to pull out that small, blue box, weighing it in my palm before carefully springing it open. I pulled the ring out of the box, admiring the geometric design of diamonds that bejeweled it. I let the stones reflect the light of the fading sun before fitting it snugly back into the box. I checked my watch. Ten minutes passed, then fifteen. Then thirty. She should have been here by now. I stood up and brushed the dirt from my pants. Anne was never late. Never. My heart raced in my chest as I reached for my bike, securing the ring back into my pocket.

Something was terribly wrong. I felt it with every ounce of my being. I raced down the hill faster than I probably should have, sweat beading above my brow as the trees created long shadows behind me. The night sky raced me as I went down the road, my wheels spurring up dust in their wake. I turned right onto Old West Side Road and pushed harder on my pedals, until I was stopped by three police cars putting up a barrier around Echo Lake. I braked hard and threw my bike to the side, then ran up to a man grasping a sign in his hands.

"What happened?" I yelled more than asked.

"Not now, James. A girl was just found dead in the lake." It was Sergeant Jacobs, a recent transfer to the Conway police station from Jackson.

"Let him through, Rob," a gravelly voice instructed.

The sergeant nodded as Inspector Evans walked closer to me, looking worse for wear.

His voice was little more than a whisper. "Anne's dead. She was just found—"

I didn't wait to hear the rest of the tragedy, and in denial I decided to run the rest of the way down the wet and sand-filled trail to the lake. Four people hovered like flies over her body, which shone paler than the stars that appeared like silver stitches in a velvet blue sky. Evans followed me, of course. He held me back as we watched her limp body get picked up and placed into a dark gray body bag. My eyes stung as I broke from Evans's grip and ran to her. I dropped to my knees, my hands shaking as I peeled back the folds of the bag to see her face. I wanted to wrap my arms around her shoulders, to hold her hand one more time. I look into her paralyzed gaze, and seeing the fear in her opened eyes sent a dagger through my heart. Why wasn't I with her? Tears fell freely from my eyes, landing on the freckles that lay scattered from her nose to her cheekbones.

"Come on, son," Inspector Evans said softly, as if he was speaking to a child.

I closed her eyes with the back of my hand and pushed her hair behind her ear. I closed my eyes and bent close to her face. "I love you," I whispered, then kissed her brow one last time.

Evans put his arm around my chest, thinking I had no more willpower in me to stand. But I had more of a fire in me than I'd ever had in my life. I burned, my heart sparking into a roaring flame. I would find out what happened and make whoever was responsible burn beside me. They would pay for what they had done. So help me God.

James placed the letter back onto the dresser, his eyes stinging as he let go of the envelope. He unbuttoned the topmost button of his shirt and pulled at the platinum chain around his neck, from which hung the same diamond ring he was going to propose to her with. He looked on the inside of the ring base: Buccellati. It was of the art deco fashion, with four geometric diamonds pointing out like a compass. James twirled the ring in his hands, knotting the chain around his neck. He would never be with her again. He would never be whole.

He changed into his pajamas and climbed into bed. Once the silence settled over him, James pulled out the ring on his chain and held it as he closed his eyes and fell asleep.

# Chapter Sixteen

James woke with a start as a fierce wind howled against the window. He groaned as he pushed himself out of bed. The thick scent of pancakes wafted from the kitchen. Wiping his eyes, he looked around for his suitcase for a fresh set of clothes. After changing, he ran his hand through his rumpled hair and left the room. James hurried down the stairs and laced his shoes.

"Ah, there you are." Evans took a puff of his pipe. "Thought I'd have to put some snow on your back to wake you up. It's already eleven." Evans opened the closet to gather James's jacket.

"Now where are you off to in such a rush?" Rose had a plate in her hand, "I'm making pancakes for a quick bite to eat. They're right off the stovetop." She showed him the plate, the pancake formed into a letter J.

The gesture tugged at his heartstrings. "Save it for me. I won't eat until I'm back." James took his coat from Evans.

"The car key is in your pocket." He stuck a thick

forefinger at him. "But if there is but one scratch," he said in warning.

"I know, I know. I'll be back when I can."

James walked down the driveway, the cold wind holding him back like long spindle fingers. He freed himself from their grasp when he entered the car, feeling the worn steering wheel before backing out and driving toward town. He flew past the evergreens, noticing how the wind weaved through their branches, causing them to shake.

He arrived in North Conway and found a parking spot outside the five-and-dime. Adrenaline poured into his veins as he exited the car, a cold sweat beading just at his hairline.

A hand clasped James's shoulder. "I didn't think you'd come." Caiden took in his son's appearance, looking him up and down before shaking his head.

James's eyes traced the hard lines and lack of color in his father's face. Caiden wore a new black suit, with a silver handkerchief to match his cane, causing the messy fabrication of who James thought his father was to be further blurred into his mind.

"How did you know it was me?" James asked.

"You're my son."

James looked into his father's green eyes; it was like looking into a mirror. "You said you wanted to talk to me. Can we just get this over with."

Caiden focused on something behind James; a trio of men standing collectively a few paces away. Suddenly, Caiden's smile wiped off his face and was replaced by the look of grave concern James remembered. His father ran his hand through his silver mane, causing it to stick up in a way that was familiar to James's own hair.

"Are you alright?"

"James, I need you to listen to me very carefully." Caiden looked over his shoulder. "I'm doing a risky thing by even seeing you. And I don't have much time. I must be going soon."

"Wait a minute. Where have you been these last, oh, I don't know, ten years? What's the reason you want to speak to me? You never wanted to talk to me before I left. Did relocating to New York City make me 'interesting' enough for you?"

Caiden shook his head. "You were never boring, James. And you definitely get your unnecessary dramatics from your mother." Caiden tightened his jacket around his large frame.

"You're avoiding the question," James said.

Caiden took a piece of paper from his coat. "Do you know who sent you this?"

"You are going through my mail?" James replied, reaching for the envelope.

Caiden brought it toward his chest. "Who knew you were coming back?"

"No one, besides yourself and Inspector Evans. What's going on? Why are you back all the sudden?"

"I had to protect you. That's why I've done everything I have. It had to be this way."

"You thought leaving would solve your issues?"

"It did, for a while."

"That's ridiculous. Things only got worse after you left." James paused. "What do you mean, for a while?"

He scratched at a small beard growing. "I just can't believe I missed someone. After your mother passed—" Caiden winced. "I had to hunt them all down. I knew they would try to get to you."

"Who?"

"The Aces."

"Who are The Aces?"

"It was a long time ago. Do you remember the case of John Windsor, the last case I worked on with Evans?"

"Evans brought it up enough, but what does that have to do with anything?"

"Everything. John Windsor was the head of The Aces. Always wore an ace solitaire ring, a sort of trophy, if you will. When we sent him to the slammer, we thought that was the end of the various organized crime around New England."

"But it wasn't?"

"No. It wasn't a strong enough case to send him away for as long as we'd hoped, so he was set free for a brief amount of time before I got him for a different case."

"Those murders, how did you know it was him?"

"That was the problem from the beginning—how to prove it was him when he had no blood on his own hands. He was a smart man, which made him even more dangerous."

"Why haven't you ever told me this before?"

"You didn't need to know then."

"And I do now? I know John Windsor died in prison a couple of years ago. I don't see how any of this is relevant."

"Things have changed. Windsor had many loyal followers in The Aces. I tried to find every man involved in his club, but I must've missed someone."

"Again, I don't understand. Why now?"

Caiden breathed heavily out of his nose. "Why do you think I cared about this case so much that I was willing to leave you for so long?"

James waited for him to answer his own question.

"The Aces killed your mother, James. And I have reason to believe they killed Anne too."

"Why them?"

"Revenge. An eye for an eye. When Windsor was first put away, they killed your mother to get back at me."

James was silent for a moment. "You told me Mom died of carbon monoxide poisoning."

"Like I could tell you what really happened. You were so young. It was the last thing you needed to hear."

James looked at the trio of men, unable to look his father in the eyes. "How was she killed?"

Caiden searched James's face for emotion but found nothing, only a mask so often used.

"Ask Evans. He was the one who found her." Caiden searched through his pockets and took out his car key.

"Wait a minute, where are you going? We need to talk about this," James said.

"I'll know when you're ready."

"Ready? Ready for what?"

"Finish your case first. Then I'm going to need your help."

"My case? What do you know about that?"

Caiden laughed. "At least that's what the paper says. Honestly, I'm surprised Evans allowed publicity so early. The press isn't the most reliable when it comes to reporting." Caiden flipped James a penny, "Go get a copy and check it out yourself. Although it's no use to frame it— whoever wrote the story spelled your name wrong at least three times." He turned to the street, the cold wind wrapping itself around them. "I'll find you when I need you."

"Sounds familiar," James mumbled, letting the wind drown him out as Caiden left.

James looked at the penny before pocketing the money and wrapping his coat tighter around himself. The cold air bit into his skin as the wind picked up. James walked to the five-and-dime. Hearing the small bell ring as he walked inside, he was immediately welcomed by the store clerk.

"I say!"

James turned to his right to find a young man laying his arms on the glass cabinet, above the hundreds of squares of fudge. "Hello Will, still stuck here?" He smiled.

Will was sixteen, with a large round face and thick curly blond hair that just barely covered his eyes. He pushed them out of the way, as if not believing that it was James before him. "You missed a good home basketball game at Kennett last night. Alden scored ten points by himself!"

James had been a referee at Kennett High School after he graduated, he liked being a part of the community that had taken care of him after his father left. "Good for him. Are you still playing then?"

"Oh yes. I've been going to the gym after work every other day, perhaps I'll get off the bench this year."

"Fingers crossed," James replied. He looked around the front of the store and found the papers stacked beside the fudge. He took one off the shelf. "I'll just be getting a paper. Thanks."

Will stretched his palm out over the counter to receive the coin. "No problem, sir!" James smiled as he opened the door to go back outside.

"Mr. Anderson?"

James let the door close in on itself before turning to match Will's gaze. "Yeah?"

"Does this mean you're going to be our division leader at camp this summer?" Will picked up a box of goods to restock the shelves.

James smiled, "We'll see if I have the patience to deal with you rascals again."

Will nodded, taking the box to the back of the store.

James looked at the front page of the paper. He saw the picture of Elizabeth boarding the station that Martin had taken, as well as a picture of Dean trailing behind Elizabeth carrying her bags. His eyes skirted across the page for the author, Martin O'Reilly, then he read as quickly as he could. There, in black and white, the story was printed. Even worse, Martin added his own theory that Clara killed Fiona and Roger killed Clara. James cursed himself as he hurried back to the borrowed car and drove to the police station. He took a deep breath before going in.

Sergeant Jacobs looked down at James. "Last I checked, you weren't a part of this police force anymore. Or did you cry to have Evans give you your job back?"

"I wouldn't dream of it."

Inspector Evans walked into the lobby, his face a flushed red. "Sergeant, don't you have a job you're supposed to be doing?" Evans put his arm around James and walked with him into his office. "James, it's a good thing you're here. We need to have a little talk." Evans closed the door and pulled down the small blinds covering the window into the lobby. "After I saw the paper, I had Jacobs pick me up." Evans shook his head. "What the Hell were you thinking." He slammed his hand onto the desk. "Don't you realize how humiliating this is? God, James. Anyone with proper sense would know not to let him publish the story." Evans threw a copy of the newspaper onto his desk.

"What could I have done to stop it? He was with me when it happened. He said he would wait to publish it," James fired back.

"And you were the fool who believed he would keep his word? Come on. Even your father knew better, and he was never one to follow the rules." He muttered something else under his breath. "Well, there isn't anything more we can do about the paper. I called Willie at *The Conway Continental* to destroy what copies they have left, but the damage is done. Alexander wants to sue Martin for the photos. Furthermore, he's convinced it was Roger who killed his wife and wants him to be hanged. After the release of the story, I wouldn't be surprised if all of Conway wanted to see that followed through."

"How did they get photos? Martin was the only one who took photos from that night and his were destroyed by light. I thought the only relevant roll was destroyed."

Evans sighed before feeling his pockets, then reached his hand out. "Can I have my car keys?"

James threw them to him. "No dents or scratches."

Evans grunted. "Good. Now, I'm going to go round up some backup and bring Alexander and Roger in for questioning." James stood to follow Evans out. "You'll be staying here, out of trouble."

James held his tongue at first, letting his frustration ebb off him as he looked around the office. "Let me help. Together we can work through it faster. We need to speak to Elizabeth, Ruth, Dean, and even Gerald too."

"I'm not going to hear another one of your ridiculous notions," Evans said.

James picked up the ring to show Evans the ring and the maze symbol engraved in it. "We need to figure out what this is a part of. What it means. For surely, this connects back to the killer or an important part of the mythology. Trust me on this. I was right about Anne, wasn't I?"

"Don't get a big head."

"Listen, in Greek mythology Selene was the personification of the moon, a sister to Helios. Selene changed her name to Elizabeth and changed her identity with it. That's why Alexander and Roger care so strongly for her; she's family."

"Saying you're right. Why then did Dean say he needed to save Selene," Evans said. "What would she need saving from? She loved Alexander and Roger. She had everything she could want."

"But she could never have them. No matter what she did, they always cared for Fiona more." James nodded. "Perhaps that night someone told her that Fiona was her mother. Perhaps it was Clara. Then she killed both Fiona and Clara for abandoning her and never telling her who she really was, making her life a lie."

"Alright. I'll bring in everyone for more questioning. But let's not jump to conclusions. If you want to keep yourself busy, log into evidence Clara's necklace and Roger's ring. Times, dates, location found. That sort of stuff."

James watched as Evans pushed his arms through the sleeves of his wool coat and arranged his red scarf. "I thought I couldn't do any work while I'm here."

Evans opened the door before turning to James, a slight tug on his lip. "You're a real headache, you know that."

James shrugged. "Just keeping up appearances."

As Evans left his office, James reached for the paper on the desk and looked at the picture of Elizabeth. In her ears were silver art deco drop earrings inlaid with onyx and diamonds to mimic dark night illuminated by a crescent moon.

After putting down the paper he looked at Evans's desk and picked up the ring that belonged to Roger, wondering where it had been made. However, as he looked at the ring, there were no engravings to indicate the maker. The ring looked soulless without its centerpiece, the engraved tridents acting as prongs toward the center. He then reached for the necklace that Clara had worn, the locket with a ruby center. James turned the locket over to find its maker but again found nothing. Both pieces of jewelry were unidentifiable.

"I'm such a moron," James whispered to himself.

# Chapter Seventeen

T he silver bell above the door rang as James entered the shop, which was only a few doors down from the station. He was met with the familiar, yet pungent smell of lavender perfume. Florence Silverstein, who was wiping down a glass cabinet, took off her thin-framed glasses to get a better look at him. Florence was the local jeweler in Conway and had opened her shop over twenty years ago. No one had thought it would thrive in the small town, but tourists flocked to her shop both in the winter and summer seasons. She was highly regarded in the community, both for her loving nature and quick wit. James had lived with her for a time after his father left him, saving him from leaving the town.

"James, I haven't seen you in ages." She clapped her hands once in delight, showing her well-manicured nails. "What's with all the radio silence? What happened to you?"

James smiled as she wrapped her arms around him in an embrace. "I just needed a change for a while."

"Of course. Here, why don't I make you a cup of tea."

Florence went through a wooden door that read **Employees Only**, then returned with a silver tray holding two cups, sugar cubes, cream, and vanilla wafers. She set it on the small coffee table that was set up for guests, along with two pink, high-backed chairs. "The tea will be out in just a moment."

"Thank you, it really isn't necessary."

"Nonsense. Those cookies have had your name written on them since the day you left."

"Hopefully not that long," he jested.

She winked. "Longer then." Her smile dipped into a frown as she looked James over. "You're here to return that ring. James, I —"

"Hold your horses there, I'm not returning anything." James tried to smile.

She relaxed, her blue eyes held their steady gaze. "What brings you here then?"

"It's about a case."

"A mystery case? Oh, I do love Sherlock Holmes," she said with excitement. "Do be kind with Mr. Evans now that you're working with him again. Lewis says he has a bad heart."

"How do you know I'm working with him?"

"News gets around." She grinned. "And Rose called this morning. Everyone in town knows you've returned."

"Nothing like being the laughingstock of the town."

"Don't be silly. We're all sorry about what happened to Anne." The tea kettle began to whistle. "I won't be gone a moment."

James looked around the familiar store and took a seat in a pink chair. Florence had set up the table and chairs by the front of the store, where large windows let people of all walks of life gaze into the rainbow assortment of gemstones. She had thought about naming her store Florence's, but settled on her last name. For her father was the one who had allowed her to pursue her career aspirations as a jeweler and businesswoman.

James looked at the sharp edges of her last name, printed on metal sheets that rested underneath the jewelry sprawled out in the window. He looked to this right to see the beige print that aligned the walls, a crown molding around the room like thick piping around a cake. Eight lightbulbs hung from the ceiling, making an L formation over the set of glass jewelry cabinets and her desk space filled with workbooks. The jewelry cabinets shined with the assortment of jewelry, arranged by name from amethyst to zircon.

James stood as Florence entered and helped her with the door as she came in with the kettle. She placed it down between them. "Here we are." She poured tea into both of their cups. "Have to keep warm these chilly January days." She put some cream into her tea and dropped two sugar cubes into James's cup. "Now, what about this case brought you to little old me?"

"I'm helping with an investigation. Some events I witnessed while coming up on *The Blue Star*. I found some jewelry, and I wonder if there is anything you could tell me about it."

"I can try." Florence grasped the handle of her cup and took it with her as she walked around to the other side of the jewelry cabinet. There, she put thin gloves on, reaching under the cabinet to take out an eyeglass.

"There are two pieces of jewelry, a ring and a locket. The ring is missing its centerpiece and the locket won't budge," James said, handing her the necklace first.

"Where did you find this?" She rolled it in her hands. "I remember this piece."

"It belonged to one of the victims," James answered honestly.

Florence picked at the grime on the clasp of the locket with her fingernail. "I wish people took better care of their jewelry. Jewelry should be worn, not shoved in pockets to be forgotten about," she remarked.

"Can you open it?" James asked, curiosity flooding through him.

"Of course I can open it," Florence said with a hint of annoyance. She went to a filing cabinet and pulled out a brown key, which looked like a miniature file. "It's just a little stuck." Florence prodded at the clasp, and with a snap, pried open the locket. James reached over the glass cabinet to get a better look, but Florence kept it close to her chest as she reached for a cyan cloth to clean the grime. Once finished, she placed the locket on the glass cabinet and smacked James's hand as he went to take it back. "Don't touch. Not yet."

James retracted his hand and nodded impatiently as Florence grabbed a large old book near the cash register.

"I keep track of every client and piece of jewelry ever made." She brought the book over to the display cabinet and carefully peeled through the fragile pages. Suddenly she stopped. "August of 1900, I sold this to a young man." She looked closer at her scrawled script. "He had the money upfront, so I didn't pester him for all his personal details."

"Is there anything else that you have on him?" James asked.

"I'm afraid not, he wanted to be anonymous."

James reached into his pocket and took out the ring he had found after discovering Fiona's murder. "What about this?"

"My goodness." Florence reached her hand out for the

ring. "It is absolutely filthy." She picked up the cleaning cloth, working on the ring. "Yes, I remember this. Fiona bought this ring on Roger's credit. I suppose they have a similar taste in gemstones, as both were made by the same jeweler."

"Can you tell who the jeweler was? I couldn't see anything on either piece."

Florence finished with the ring and held both pieces in her hand. "Of course. I follow the jewelry trends as they come and go." She thought for a moment. "Both pieces are fine platinum from a collection created in New York. Not many were produced or sold in this style. This collection was known as *Couronne des Étoiles*. Crown of Stars. It was presented at the gallery with this name due to its brightness, a nod to Selene or Luna, the Greek and Roman personifications of the moon."

James watched as Florence examined the gemstone that came out of the necklace and then took a tool to pinch the springs to fit it back in the ring. "The bonds kept it intact, although someone tried to open it. See the small scratches along the base?"

James nodded. "Could a letter opener make that kind of scratch?"

"Possibly. It would leave a mark because the blade would be too thick to open the bonds."

"What could have been so important inside of a locket?" James asked.

"Let's see then. Hmm?" Florence unhinged the top and bottom and pressed against the edges with her fingers, then handed the piece over the counter to James.

James looked at the engraving. "What does it say?" James asked.

Florence handed him the eyepiece and locket so he could look for himself.

Dean Helios Cross - October 25th, 1897

Selene Elizabeth Cross - July 12th, 1900

Florence closed her book and put it away, wiping her eyeglass piece with another cloth. "Did that help at all?"

"Yes, it does. Thank you." He picked up the locket and put it back in his pocket. "Sun and moon," James whispered to himself. "That's it. That's why it happened on the solar eclipse. Dean saw himself as the sun, the all-seer, and on a total solar eclipse the moon blocked the sun." James's eyes went wide.

She picked up her cup of tea. "Come, finish your tea before you go."

But her words fell on deaf ears, as James was already halfway out the door.

# Chapter Eighteen

The wind whipped Evans's hair as he unlocked his car and took a seat. While he waited for the passenger to arrive, he wiped the tiredness from his eyes. Soon, the man came out and opened the door in one swift motion, shaking the car as the door slammed behind him. Evans turned the key in the ignition, then pulled out from the parking spot and onto the ice-glazed roads.

Evans muttered something inaudible to himself as Caiden leaned back into the passenger seat.

"Evans," Caiden said in acknowledgement, rubbing his hands together to keep himself warm.

"Anderson."

"There is a lot behind Jack's General Market we can go to."

Evans respected his instructions, as that was the way they'd gone many nights ago, and parked into the abandoned lot. Giant pine trees stood guard over the car, blocking it from view to anyone in the bar across the street.

He followed Caiden as they walked toward Hexate. "I never thought we would go back to this miserable joint."

Caiden stopped at the entrance, which had a small line outside. "I wish we didn't have to. I thought we ended their regime years ago."

"A vendetta like this will never rest," Evans said.

"We should have warned them."

"When Windsor got sent down, everyone thought they were done. It's not our fault."

"Fool's hope. And I'm not saying it is them, but we should have known better."

When the doors opened to receive them, the line of people flooded into the violet lounge. The lovely ladies were dressed in a sea of color, from elegant reds to breathtaking greens and transcending blues. Every color was represented in shades matching the darker themes of the night. The gentlemen were clad in suits. One gentleman had long whiskers that cascaded over his hazel brown pipe. Smoke rose from the crowd toward the lights hanging from the gilded ceiling, creating a cloud over the guests.

Caiden entered first, his eyes quickly adjusting to the dim lighting as he casually walked through the party mongers. "I can't believe this is the same place." He turned to Evans, who looked around the club, catching glimpses of the Greek mythology referenced throughout, including a moon emblazoned by the stage. Caiden stopped at a round table with a white tablecloth and candle in the middle.

"Look who we have here. I never thought our own Caiden Anderson would find his way back here. What can I do for ya?" A large man stood before the two of them, his red cheeks glowing. He laughed as he wrapped his fat sausage-like fingers around Caiden's shoulder. "Good to see you. Very good."

"Don. How have you been?" Caiden said.

"Oh, just dandy. Is there anything I can get for you?"

"I think I'll have a coffee, black."

Don looked to Evans. "Anything for you, sir?"

Evans cleared his throat. "Nothing for me."

"Hey, Don," Caiden said. "Could I speak to the boss for a second?"

"No can do, pals. The boss man is away. Why'd you want to do that anyhow?"

"We're looking for Miss Kingston."

Don laughed. "Oh, everybody is after her today. Nasty business. The bosses got her some gig in Boston for the time being. She's at an appointment tonight." His smile faded. "Probably shouldn't have told ya that."

Loud music bounced off the cushioned walls. "We appreciate the honesty, Don. We're only here to help," Evans said. "Busy night tonight?"

"Yup. We're all packed in tight, like sardines or something similar. But there's always room for you two."

"Who manages the place when the boss is gone?" Caiden asked.

"Used to be a young fellow, but he's going with Elizabeth to Boston." He heard a hiss as another server passed him. "I'll be back with your drinks soon," he added.

Once the pressure left his shoulders, Caiden stretched his back and heard it crack.

"I didn't know you knew Don," Evans said, scanning the fellow as he went back to the kitchens.

"Well, he and I went to the same school for a time. That is, before he was forced to drop out. His father didn't really approve of educating him, thought it was pointless.

He comes from a family of painters. Don didn't like the smell, made him sneeze." Caiden smiled.

Don came lumbering back soon enough. "Here they are, coffee and a whole lot of nothing. Y'know, Caiden, coffee isn't the best for yer health. Must think of your heart."

Caiden waved his hand. "Some say black coffee is good for the heart."

Evans changed the topic. "Hey, what happened to Salty's that was here before?"

"It's really been that long, huh?" Don scratched his head. "The Old Salt Box closed ten years ago. Hexate has been open ever since. The boss was kind enough to rehire the same staff... if they were able to keep their mouths shut."

"The entire staff?" Evans repeated.

Don nodded. "Yup, even old Grubby, God help him. Not much has changed besides the interior and all that frilly, girly stuff. Same food, same drink. Made the job easier for me. Except for the lounge downstairs for the speakeasy, that was an addition. Boss calls it Elysium. That's where Elizabeth usually stays. She performs every other night. Not that she's very good, in my opinion. No, it's pretty clear what's keeping us afloat this time around instead of with Salty, but I don't give a hoot who runs the place as long as I get paid." Don clapped Caiden on the back.

The lights went out and the smooth jazz on stage abruptly stopped. A floodlight from the back of the bar sparked a beam of light that danced against the downtrodden chestnut stage. There were silver curtains aligned on either side, with a hand-carved mantle beaming overhead. Chattering broke out among the crowd. When the curtains parted, a man stepped out of the crease in the curtain. The man was in navy blue and white pin-striped pants with a blue blazer, a square handkerchief in his right breast pocket. His glowing green eyes became more vibrant as the light struck him. His greased hair stood up like soldiers, as if trying to detach themselves from the ghoulish smile below his abnormally large nose.

"It is my honor to introduce Jezebel. She will be singing in place of Elizabeth Kingston tonight."

Don shouldered Evans roughly. "I think she's a heck of a lot better. You'll see."

Jezebel walked out in a long violet dress that moved in waves as she strode toward the platform to begin her enchantment. She wore dark rounded sunglasses and a silver bobbed hairstyle. The room was deathly quiet, almost as if everyone was afraid to breathe and potentially disturb the tranquility. She let out a shrill laugh. "I hope you all enjoy my song, my friends."

Caiden moved closer to Don, who shushed him and continued listening, pulling up a chair and putting his thick arms on their table.

Evans waited for the song to end, looking around the room till it was over. He scrutinized the mantle, specifically the full moon residing in the middle, with two reflecting crescents on either side. Inside the moon was a pinwheel-looking shape with six sides, a rounded maze flowing around it. His eyes widened as he remembered the symbol James had shown him.

Caiden downed his coffee and used another server to order another one.

Evans looked out at the audience before turning back to look at Don, reevaluating him.

"What is it with this place?" Caiden asked Don.

"It is called Hexate for a reason. Hecate was the Goddess of magic, the moon, crossroads, and necromancy.

Her symbol is on the mantel." Don pointed to the large full moon and matching crescents. "If there is something Dean and Roger have in common, it is their attachment to Greek mythology. They say we're all connected to it somehow. I don't believe none of it, but don't tell Dean I said that. He's always going on about Hades and the abduction of Persephone, bless him."

"Sounds like an interesting man. Might we have a word with him?" Caiden asked.

"He was," Don started. "He was kind of the heart and soul of this place. Found entertainment, stirred up new drinks, he cared about all of us. In his own way."

"Is he here?" added Evans.

Don shook his head, "I'm afraid not. Dean stopped by after he got off that train that came through the other day. Said he was never going to return to us after his falling out with Kingston."

"Don, bring me a drink," Jezebel called out as she walked out from the stage and made her way to the bar.

"Yes, ma'am." Don looked at Caiden and Evans. "Well, I should probably get back there and help 'em out with the drinks. If you're looking for any of the owners, they've all fled. It'll be like finding a needle in a haystack. I wouldn't go looking for them though, you don't want to end up the same way that girl did."

"What girl? Was she a worker here?"

Don shrugged. "She was another one of 'em singers. She cozied up to Elizabeth, Alexander, and Roger plenty, but especially Dean. She was a part of his fantasy with all those books. See, she always carried around a copy of that *Wonderland* book. Practically obsessed with it. Wasn't until Dean got a look at it that it was curtains for her. Awful luck. Beautiful girl."

Evans reached over the table to grab Don by the shirt.

"Easy there." Caiden pushed himself out of his chair.

Don's eyes widened. "Hey, knock it off. I meant her no offense if you knew her. She had a bit of a reputation, that's all."

Caiden stood and walked to the other side of the table. "Don, shut up."

"What's taking so long?" Jezebel yelled across the crowd to Don.

"Come on, Evans, we have to go. We're making a scene." Caiden hit Evans's arm until he released Don.

Don fixed his shirt, turning to Caiden. "Do you remember that inquiry about the missing girl, from the drunkard?"

Caiden furrowed his brow. "The fake report. Sure, why?"

Don looked around the room. "If you're up for the challenge. It wouldn't hurt to pay that place a visit tonight. If you know what I mean."

# Chapter Nineteen

James found the old farmhouse on 15 Continental surrounded in its own burrow of nature. Windows had fallen into disrepair, the door was falling off its hinges, and snow covered the roof. A creaking gate sang as the wind pushed it back and forth, a haunting melody from the croaking iron disrupting the deafening silence. Laying his bike on the snow, James approached the door. He grasped the knob and the door came free from its hinges. Placing the broken door against the wall, James entered the house. He turned the light switch on, and the bulb flickered once before popping. James felt in his right pant pocket for a match to light instead. The naked flame licked at his fingers as it danced in the darkness, illuminating the silver threaded cobwebs that held the house together. He lit the gas lights that still stood on the walls. As he shook the flame to sleep, he heard floorboards creak behind him.

Adrenaline flooded his veins. He spun around and saw the shadow of a figure lunge toward him, arm raised.

"Surprised?" Dean laughed, his tongue lashing against

his lip. He used his weight to push the knife he held closer to James.

"Where's Selene?" James yelled, pushing the knife away from his face.

Dean pulled back, and the sudden change of direction caused James to stumble toward the wall.

"Where is Selene?" James asked again, seeing Elizabeth's white coat across a beaten-down green couch behind Dean.

Dean's dark eyes jumped with excitement. "Wouldn't you like to know," he replied nonchalantly.

James looked at the knife, thicker than the letter opener and sanguine with blood. He was unable to tell if the blood was fresh. James's mind reeled as Dean came on him again. James shuffled to the left, elbowing his arm and knocking the blade out of his hand.

"Quick reflexes," Dean said condescendingly. "I'm both impressed and flattered that you stuck with me this long. It might just be the most attention I've ever gotten. If only your friend Martin was here to write it all down. Pity you won't be seeing his name printed in the paper anymore." Dean grinned as James's jaw tightened. "Don't worry, I didn't hurt him. I wouldn't dream of it after everything he has done for me. Everything you have done for me."

James kept his eyes on Dean as he picked up the blade, then pointed it at Dean. "What have I done for you?"

Dean smiled, his face aglow. "Why, you made me famous. Almost like my sister. For once, what I did will be in black and white. I will be remembered, my name forever attached to theirs. Everyone will know their shame."

"Why did you spare Roger? Why was it Clara and Fiona who had to die?"

"Roger never knew about me. My mother and Clara

didn't tell him. When I went home after the war, my adoptive parents told me everything." Dean huffed. "Fiona didn't care about me, and so she had to pay for her sin. For her pride." He smiled a chilling smile that looked like it had been painted on in acrylic. "This was all my mother's fault. If she didn't have that silly affair this wouldn't have happened. She deserves everything that came her way. She will burn in Hell."

James looked at him carefully. "No one deserves to die, and whether they live or not is not a choice for you to make. And to have her die so painfully. Why?"

"I didn't want my poor old mother to forget," Dean recounted bitterly. "To forget that wretched day she brought Selene into the world. I thought maybe if they remembered Selene, they would remember me. I figured you would find out the date and this could fall on Roger. Nothing you can do will change what happens. Roger and Alexander have run away, cowards that they are. Making them seem all the more guilty. The paper says they will accuse Roger of both Fiona's and Clara's murders. It will be a full circle."

"If Roger is accused, then no one will know that you did this? The world they live in is full of stigma and social etiquette and expectations. They had to send you away to keep you safe from being branded a bastard child in the press. Living life with that black mark was a life neither of them wanted you to have," said James.

"You lie so tastefully," Dean mocked. The tips of his mouth rose into a smile. "Her reputation mattered to her more than her own son." He paused, then shook his index finger. "My own mother threw me out the day I was born like I was nothing, and Clara enabled it. That's why they had to die, to pay for this." He gestured toward himself. "You don't know what it's like to be abandoned. To feel like no one cares if you lived or died. When I was in the war, I had nothing to lose. My brothers in combat who died on the battlefield had mothers, fathers, sisters, and lovers to return to, but my life was meaningless. Yet I was spared."

"What about Selene? You thought about coming back for her. You said you had a tattoo of a sun and moon put on your skin when you were in the war," James said.

"I was a fool to believe in her. To think that she would remember me. Everyone loved the perfect Selene. She was so gracious and loving, not burning with hate."

James wanted to keep him talking, to find out about Selene. "You told Selene you could run away together. That was the note Clara found. It wasn't from Roger. It was from you. You knew she would be on the train working with Roger, and when you reintroduced yourself to her, she didn't remember you."

Dean sneered. "I didn't expect her to remember me. Not at first. But when I told her my plan, she thought I was crazy and called me a liar. She didn't want to face the truth. She'd rather live a beautiful lie with those snakes. Clara was blackmailing Roger, threatening to tell the public about Elizabeth's true story. To think! Then Chief Michaels handpicks a journalist and you, a ditzy detective, to be with us. Made it easier than pie to reveal the truth, to have my revenge."

James furrowed his brow. "Those numbers on Fiona's arm—71200. July 12th, 1900. That's Selene's birthday, isn't it? Why did you write her birthday?"

Dean smiled, seeing his reflection in the knife. "Isn't it obvious? I hated who she became. The Selene I used to love was dead. Now she was just the moon that blocked the sun. She was the total eclipse that brought on destruction and disaster. Selene is finally dead, and so is the faker,

Elizabeth. Now, I have control. For once, all the attention is on me."

He rolled up his sleeve and showed his sun tattoo. "Don't you see? I am Helios. The all-seeing God. Selene got everything I never could have: closeness with the family, attention, wealth, power. I saw it all happen. I saw everything happen and I knew the truth. My family was living a fantasy while I was suffocating on reality. Now they will all pay their due." Dean daydreamed for a second before turning his attention back to James. "I'm sure you know how this has to end."

Dean pounced on James. "It's nothing personal. Just. Hold. Still." He kneed James in the ribs which caused him to drop the dagger and clutch his chest. Dean was quick as he picked up the dagger that dropped and buried the blade into James's side. Dean huffed. "Not so quick now, are you?"

James fell as Dean pulled the blade out. Sticky crimson blood coated James's hands as he held his wound, saturating his white shirt as his knees buckled under him.

"That's your problem," Dean said. "You're always just a hair behind. Behind Fiona, Clara, Elizabeth. Even your precious Anne. I knew Anne, another liar who didn't know what she was getting herself into."

James felt the adrenaline kick in as he found his footing and pushed Dean against the wall, his hands about Dean's throat. "What do you know about her?" he said, a glob of saliva trailing down the side of his mouth.

Dean shoved against James's chest, causing James to fall and land on his back and hit the back of his head. Dean stood over James and kicked him in the side. "Look at you, you're pathetic. You're not as sharp as she was by half. A pity that she played her cards wrong. That she had faith in you."

Dean circled around James, like a panther playing with his prey. "I suppose the game ends here for us." He pointed the knife at James triumphantly. "The curtain closes on this case." He paused, and the silence was deafening. "Then again, if you're dead and gone, who is left to find out the truth about Anne's story? I think I'd like to see you try." Dean slowly turned the knife toward himself. "I think it's my time to go, let everyone else live in the wake of this nightmare." Once he had done it, his body felt limp as he fell next to James on the floor.

James forced air into his lungs, but felt his cheeks grow numb and then his fingers. His vision ebbed from dark to light, while a high pitch rang in his ears. The fuzzy warmth of car headlights shone through the cracked windows.

"James." Inspector Evans lumbered over to him, grabbing James under the arms to pull him up on to his feet. Evans threw one of James's arms over his shoulder and helped him outside to the waiting ambulance.

James struggled to think. "How did you know I was here?"

"No questions for now, James. Just try to breathe. It's going to be okay. Alright?"

James gasped. "It was Dean. He's Roger and Fiona's son. He said —"

"James, we will get it sorted," Evans said as he helped him get into the ambulance. "Your health is the most important thing right now."

James heard voices all around him, but it was hard to concentrate. Slowly, the light faded into nothingness.

# Chapter Twenty

A hazy, golden light was the first thing James saw when his eyes fluttered open in the hospital. He winced as he sat up in the bed he was on, grabbing his left side. James started to swing his legs over the side of the bed but stopped after the movement took too much out of him. After settling back in bed, he noticed the white chrysanthemums on the bedside table with a small card.

*Feel Better Soon! Lots of Love, Mr. and Mrs. Evans*

James could tell it was written by Rose due to her large, swirling script. Just like Anne's. She also always sprayed a lavender and peony perfume on her notes. He placed the card next to him in bed and reached for the newspaper that lay underneath the card.

DEAN BRADLEY COMMITS DOUBLE
HOMICIDE; KILLS SELF RATHER THAN
FACE CHARGES

Disgust spread like a disease across James's face. Dean ended up getting the attention and publicity he craved. He sighed, closing the paper.

Inspector Evans let himself into the room. "James. You really had us all worried." He sighed in relief as he took a few paces toward James. There was the sound of nails scratching at the polished floor, and James looked down to find Winston leading Evans through the door. As Winston picked up the familiar scent of James, he launched himself onto the bed.

"Slow down there, buddy," Evans said, reaching for the small dog's collar.

James smiled as he reached to scratch Winston's ears, the dog obliviously sitting on his chest.

"Oh, get down." The inspector snapped to get the dog's attention, and Winston slightly moved closer to James's good side and curled up under his arm. Winston stuck out his long pink tongue in appreciation as James patted his small head.

"They're going to have your head for bringing Winston here," James said, a mischievous smile tugging at his lips.

Evans shrugged. "They'll be alright." He moved his way to the bed and sat down beside James. "I suppose you're wondering what happened to the Cross brothers and Elizabeth?"

James looked at him, gesturing for him to continue.

"They were all cleared, of course. Elizabeth told her story to the press on her own terms, and they gobbled it up. So really, no harm done there."

James snickered. "I suppose Alexander was right in saying no press is bad press."

"That's a tall tale if I ever heard one. Willie does a good job of letting me know in advance if something is coming out we might not like, but the rest of them are slippery folk." He chuckled before settling into a sigh. "You were right about Anne, of course. Sometimes it felt like you and Rose knew her better than I did."

James's heart grew heavy as he looked at Evans, his shoulders slouching over as if weighed down.

"I just didn't want her to hang around clubs and saloons. Well, you know. People are dangerous when they're in groups. You never know who could be connected to who. My Anne. I was the luckiest man in the world to be her father. She could do anything if she put her mind to it. I know she could have been in the police force, but I wanted to protect her from it." Evans took a deep breath. "Listen, I need to apologize." He looked to the door and then back at James. "I should have stood up for you back when—"

"It's okay." James bit the side of his cheek. "It's fine."

"No, it's not." The inspector put a hand on James's shoulder. "The fumbling of Anne's case, isolating you, none of it was okay. I swear one day I'll make it up to you. I can only do what I can with the time I have now to fix everything. But I need you to help. You're the only one in our midst who saw right through it."

"Get to the point already, Charlie. The boy needs to know." A figure emerged from the shadows of the doorframe.

Evans stood beside the bed as Caiden came closer. "Patience has never been your strong suit."

"And you've always liked your riddles and roundabout conclusions," Caiden said.

"Inspector Evans."

The Inspector turned his head to see the nurse frowning at him. Evans nodded, picking up Winston and placing him on the floor. He turned back to James. "Feel better, James. I'll catch up with you both later." He looked at Caiden in contempt before walking toward the nurse, the little dog's nails clicking on the floor.

James arched his brow as he looked back at his father. "Didn't think I'd ever see the two of you together again."

"I wouldn't have believed it either." Caiden walked closer to James's side. "But with Anne's case, it's clear someone close to the force is involved. The autopsy report is missing and Anne's case file was destroyed."

James pulled himself up from the bed. "We need to reopen the case then, find out who got in and destroyed her report."

Caiden pushed against James's shoulder to have him lie back down. "That's easier said than done. If we're going to pursue this case, we need to do this on our own. Keep everything close to chest." He looked at Evans, who was speaking to the nurse just outside the door.

Reaching into his jacket pocket, he pulled out a thin envelope and handed it to James. "I found this in the woods around Echo Lake the day Anne was killed."

James took the envelope into his hands and felt the edge of the delicate paper. Sweet perfume still lingered. He looked up at the stern face of his father. "How did you get this? They combed the woods for hours and found nothing. When were you here?" James opened the letter, gently lifting the flap to pull out the scribbles that danced along the page. "Why give this to me now?"

"It wasn't time. But with the Hexate club coming back into the limelight, perhaps we can put things to bed once and for all. Anne knew about the club; she knew about all of it." He paused for a moment, pulling at his sleeves. "And I believe that knowledge is what got her killed."

# About the Author

Samantha Sudol is a recent graduate of the University of Maine, where she earned her bachelor's degree in English and Psychology. During her studies, Samantha was honored with several awards, including the Abby Sargent Neese Kelly Creative Writing Scholarship, the Nellie Ruth Pillsbury King Memorial Scholarship, and the Center for Undergraduate Research (CUGR) Fellowship. In addition to her love of writing, Samantha is an avid reader with interests in history, mythology and folklore. Besides her passion for literature, Samantha enjoys traveling and watching the latest true crime shows. She currently resides in New Jersey and will soon be pursuing a Master's degree in Literary Studies at the University of Exeter.